NOTHING MOVED.

The incoming tide had washed him up onto the beach and left him there as it receded. Now, he lay on his back in the pale darkness and gazed sightlessly up at the moon, while the declining ocean washed over his Air Jordans.

He lay like that in the stillness of death until morning, when a yellow Labrador retriever trotted happily down the beach and stopped to sniff at him. She wagged her tail and stepped back a little, then began to circle him, sniffing as she went, her tail wagging eagerly. A ways behind the dog came her owner, a woman wearing a Red Sox baseball cap and a maroon warm-up suit. She carried a leash. When she saw her dog sniffing, the woman stopped.

"Molly," she said to the dog, her voice beginning to rise. "Molly, you get away from there. Molly! Molly!"

#

OTHER BOOKS YOU MAY ENJOY

The Angel of Death: *A Forensic Mystery*	Alane Ferguson
Black Duck	Janet Taylor Lisle
The Christopher Killer: *A Forensic Mystery*	Alane Ferguson
The Circle of Blood: *A Forensic Mystery*	Alane Ferguson
Edenville Owls	Robert B. Parker
First Shot	Walter Sorrells
Hunted: Fake ID	Walter Sorrells
Rat Life	Tedd Arnold
Something Rotten: *A Horatio Wilkes Mystery*	Alan M. Gratz
The Sword That Cut *the Burning Grass*	Dorothy & Thomas Hoobler

Robert B. Parker

THE BOXER AND THE SPY

SLEUTH

S P E A K

An Imprint of Penguin Group (USA) Inc.

SPEAK SLEUTH
Published by the Penguin Group
Penguin Young Readers Group, 345 Hudson Street, New York, New York 10014, U.S.A.
Penguin Group (Canada), 90 Eglinton Avenue East, Suite 700, Toronto, Ontario, Canada M4P 2Y3
(a division of Pearson Penguin Canada Inc.)
Penguin Books Ltd, 80 Strand, London WC2R 0RL, England
Penguin Ireland, 25 St Stephen's Green, Dublin 2, Ireland (a division of Penguin Books Ltd)
Penguin Group (Australia), 250 Camberwell Road, Camberwell, Victoria 3124, Australia
(a division of Pearson Australia Group Pty Ltd)
Penguin Books India Pvt Ltd, 11 Community Centre,
Panchsheel Park, New Delhi - 110 017, India
Penguin Group (NZ), 67 Apollo Drive, Rosedale, North Shore 0632, New Zealand
(a division of Pearson New Zealand Ltd)
Penguin Books (South Africa) (Pty) Ltd, 24 Sturdee Avenue,
Rosebank, Johannesburg 2196, South Africa

Registered Offices: Penguin Books Ltd, 80 Strand, London WC2R 0RL, England

First published in the United States of America by Philomel Books,
a division of Penguin Young Readers Group, 2008
This Sleuth edition first published by Speak, an imprint of Penguin Group (USA) Inc., 2009

3 5 7 9 10 8 6 4

THE LIBRARY OF CONGRESS HAS CATALOGED THE PHILOMEL BOOKS EDITION AS FOLLOWS:
Parker, Robert B., date
The boxer and the spy / Robert B. Parker.
p. cm.
Summary: Fifteen-year-old Terry, an aspiring boxer, uncovers the mystery
behind the unexpected death of a classmate.
ISBN: 978-0-399-24775-0 (hc)
[1. Mystery and detective stories. 2. Boxing—Fiction.] I. Title.
PZ7.P2346Bo 2008 [Fic]—dc22 2007023689

Speak /Sleuth ISBN 978-0-14-241439-2

Printed in the United States of America

Designed by Katrina Damkoehler

For Joan, who needs no blue butterfly.

THE BOXER
AND THE SPY

SKYCAM I

Twenty miles north of Boston, Cabot was a rich town on the water. The houses were generally big and old and had nice yards. Along the ocean-front, on Water Street, the houses were mostly bigger and older and had long front porches where people could sit in good weather and look at the ocean.

The boy liked to walk around town after dark and look in windows. He liked to see the lives being lived in the lighted interiors. Men reading newspapers, women making supper, kids doing homework. He didn't peek in, he just looked as he walked by and felt somehow comfortable looking at the regular people doing regular things. He didn't like to stay home so much after supper because ever since his father died, his mother wouldn't eat supper. She'd give him his and sit with him while he ate, and drink. In a little while she would get weeping and hug him and tell him he was all she had, and it would make him really uncomfortable. So he'd go out for a walk until she got so drunk she'd fall asleep on the couch. He had gotten the timing of it down pretty well, so when he came home, he could go right to bed. In the morning there would be no mention of it. The boy didn't have too many friends. He wasn't mean or anything, but a lot of kids thought he was a sissy because he didn't like sports, and he liked old movies, and he liked to draw. He knew that, but he couldn't change himself. He could only be what he was.

There was a sort of closed-in space on the beach, at the far end, near the bathhouse, among the big smooth rocks that stuck out into the ocean, where the boy liked to sit sometimes and think about things, and wait for his mother to drink herself to sleep. It was a cloudy night, but warm for March, and the boy was comfortable in the shadows of his place in the rocks.

A man and woman walked along the beach toward his rocks. They walked close together.

"It's okay?" the man said.

"Absolutely," the woman said.

"The property is in my name?"

"Yes."

"Even though it's a school project," the man said.

"Yes. Cost will simply be subsumed in the school budget," the woman said.

"And the fact that it's on conservation land?"

"That particular parcel," the woman said, "is no longer conservation land."

"How'd you do that?"

"You know the right buttons to push," she said, "you don't have to push many in a town like this."

The boy sank as low as he could in his place. There was no moon showing. Thank god it was cloudy.

The man and woman had stopped and stood perhaps three feet from the boy, above the high water line, looking out over the dark ocean.

"It'll stand up?" the man said.

"It'll stand up and the way is greased for the next project and the one after that," the woman said.

"Did it cost us?"

"Money? No. We don't have to split the money with anyone. I scratched some backs, they scratched mine. I know how this town runs."

"You ought to," the man said. "You run it."

"I do," she said.

"What do you think we can sell the house for?"

"My guess, a million eight," she said.

"Nine hundred thousand each," he said. "And how much did it cost us?"

She laughed softly.

"Nothing," she said, and turned and kissed him hard on the mouth. They held the kiss, and then slowly separated.

"Give me a few minutes," she said. "If people

saw us coming from the beach together, at this
time of night, they might get the wrong idea."

The man laughed.

"And they'd be right," he said.

. She laughed and patted his cheek and turned
and walked away down the beach. He watched
her as she went. The clouds that had hidden the
moon drifted so that he could see her in the moonlight as she turned up the path and walked
toward the street where they had parked sepa-
rately. The moonlight seemed to the boy as bright as
day. The man turned back and looked directly
at the boy. Their eyes met.

"You," the man said. "You were there. . . ."

The boy was frozen. He could hear the heavy
rasp of the man's breath.

"You heard everything," the man said.

"I didn't hear anything," the boy said.

"Yeah," the man said. "You did."

CHAPTER 1

Keep your shoulder up," George said, "and turn your hand so you hitting like with the first two knuckles."

Terry nodded. He was wearing sneakers and knee-length black shorts and a blue tank top. George held up the big padded mitts.

"Left foot forward," George said. "Stay balanced. Knees bent. Push against the floor."

Terry nodded.

"Left jab," George said, "left jab, right cross."

"Two lefts," Terry said.

"Yep. Crisp. Make his head snap."

Terry went into his stance. His hands and wrists were taped. Over the tape, he had on big blue boxing gloves. He put the left one up near his temple and the right one a little lower, near the hinge of his jaw. His left foot was forward. He shuffled forward slightly and jabbed with his left, torquing his forearm so the punch would land the first two knuckles. And again. Both punches were off-center and slid off the mitt without the satisfying pop you got when it was solid.

"Set up," George said.

Back to his stance briefly, then the right cross. It popped into George's left mitt. Better.

"The jabs sucked," Terry said.

"They were good punches," George said. "They would have done the job. They just didn't hit the sweet spot."

"Right cross was there," Terry said.

"Supposed to be," George said. "Let's do it again."

"Same thing?"

"Same thing."

They did it again, and three more times. Terry never got all three punches right in sequence.

"Take a break," George said, and nodded at a folding chair.

"What the hell is wrong with me?" Terry said. "I can't get it."

George smiled. "How old are you?" he asked.

"Fifteen," Terry said.

"Not too late," George said. "I think you got time to learn."

"We been working at it for two months now," Terry said.

"Take three, four thousand punches, each punch, 'fore you groove the muscle memory," George said.

"How many you think I've done?"

"'Bout three hundred," George said.

Terry worked on his breathing. He still couldn't believe how hard it was to box, how tired he got, how quick.

"How many you think you've done, George?"

George smiled and squinched his eyes and tilted his head back as if he were figuring.

"A million," he said. "And eight."

"Eight," Terry said.

George was a solid-looking black man, with a modest potbelly and graying hair. He shuffled his feet a little and put a tight left hook into the heavy bag. The bag nearly came loose from its tether.

"Nine," George said.

They both laughed.

"Doesn't that hurt your hand?" Terry said.

"Nope."

"You're not wearing gloves, you're not even taped. Why doesn't it hurt?"

"Used to it," George said.

He was wearing black sweatpants and a gray T-shirt. His arms were still muscular looking.

"How old are you, George?" Terry said.

"Fifty-five."

"How long did you fight?"

"Started when I was a kid, quit when I was forty-one."

"Did you start doing this right after?" Terry said.

"Nope."

"So what'd you do?"

"I sparred a little, did some work as a bouncer."

"Ever lose a fight in a bar?"

"Didn't have many," George said. "Ones I had didn't last very long."

"But did you ever lose?"

"No," George said. "'Course not."

Terry nodded. His breathing had steadied.

"Round two?" he said.

"Round two," George said. "You and the heavy bag."

His name was Jason Green and he was dead. The incoming tide had washed him up onto the beach and left him there as it receded. Now, he lay on his back in the pale darkness and gazed sightlessly up at the moon, while the declining ocean washed over his Air Jordans.

He lay like that in the stillness of death until morning, when a yellow Labrador retriever trotted happily down the beach and stopped to sniff at him. She wagged her tail and stepped back a little, then began to circle him, sniffing as she went, her tail wagging eagerly. A ways behind the dog came her owner, a woman wearing a Red Sox baseball cap and a maroon warm-up suit.

She carried a leash. When she saw her dog sniffing, the woman stopped.

"Molly," she said to the dog, her voice beginning to rise. "Molly, you get away from there. Molly! Molly!"

Molly stopped sniffing and looked at her owner.

"Molly," the owner was screaming now. "You come, now! Come!"

Molly gave the dog equivalent of a resigned shrug and trotted over to the woman in the maroon warm-ups. The woman snapped the leash onto Molly's collar and turned, and the two of them ran back up the beach. As they ran, Molly looked back now and then. Her owner did not.

The morning sun was bright. It dried the wet clothes the boy was wearing. The ocean water was very calm. The tide had ebbed entirely during the night, and turned, and was now beginning imperceptibly to creep in. A few gulls landed near the body and hopped around, looking at it. Nothing else moved.

After a time, in the distance, there was the sound of a siren. Then a police car pulled up in the beach parking lot, and two cops got out and walked down the beach toward the body. When the cops got close, the gulls began to squawk and then flew up and circled overhead while the cops squatted in the sand beside the dead boy.

CHAPTER 2

"Did you hear about Jason?" Abby said.

They were hanging on the Wall across from the town common.

"Jason Green?" Terry said.

"Yes," Abby said. "He committed suicide."

Terry stared at her.

"Suicide?"

"Yeah," Tank said. "Cops said he loaded up on 'roids and it made him crazy."

"Steroids?" Terry said.

"Isn't it awful?" Beverly said.

"Jason never did 'roids," Terry said. "He wasn't a jock. He wanted to be some kind of damn landscape designer."

"They found him on the beach," Suzi said.

She seemed excited. Her cheeks were bright.

"They said he probably jumped off the Farragut Bridge and the currents took him to our beach," Suzi said. "Some woman found him when she was walking her dog."

Beverly hunched her shoulders and hugged herself as if she were cold.

"How'd you like to have found him?" she said.

"How come you haven't heard about this?" Abby asked. "It was on the tube last night. It was all over school today."

Terry shrugged.

"All Terry thinks about is boxing," Suzi said.

"And sex," Terry said.

"With Abby?" Suzi said.

"I don't know what he's thinking about," Abby said. "He sure isn't doing anything."

"Not because I don't try," Terry said.

They all laughed. Suzi took out a pack of long thin cigarettes and lit one.

"Try me," Suzi said.

They all laughed again.

"Abby can't fight me off forever," Terry said.

"Don't count on it," Abby said, and smiled at Terry.

"You ever take anything?" Tank said. "You know, to help with the boxing and stuff?"

Terry shook his head.

"George would kick my butt right out of the gym if he caught me," Terry said.

"You really going for the Golden Gloves?" Terry said.

"Not this year, maybe next, depends on when George thinks I'm ready."

"Was he really a pro boxer?" Tank said.

"George fought everybody," Terry said.

"So how come he's in some little health club teaching kids?" Suzi said.

"Probably didn't beat everybody," Tank said.

"He beat a lot," Terry said.

A tan Ford Fusion cruised past the common and stopped in front of the Wall.

"I think that's the principal," Beverly said.

The side window went down. It was Mr. Bullard.

"Get rid of the cigarette," he said.

He was a thick man, with a thick neck.

"We're not in school," Tank said.

"Get rid of it," Mr. Bullard said.

"Yes sir, Mr. Principal," Suzi said.

She dropped the cigarette on the sidewalk and carefully stamped it out. Bullard nodded, looked hard at Tank for a moment, and drove away. As soon as he was out of sight, Suzi took out another cigarette and lit it.

"You know," Beverly said, "I think, actually, it's against the law. I think they passed it last year."

"Smoking?" Suzi asked.

"Smoking in a public place," Beverly said.

"That's bogus," Tank said.

They all sat watching the smoke from Suzi's cigarette curl up into the soft air.

"Who says Jason was on 'roids?" Terry asked.

"It was on TV last night," Terry said.

"So that makes it true for sure," Suzi said.

"Yeah, babe," Tank said. "If there's one thing you can trust, it's television."

"They did an autopsy," Suzi said.

"And they found some kind of note," Beverly added.

"What'd it say?" Terry asked.

"I don't know. They just said it was a suicide note."

"Jason was kind of porky," Tank said. "Maybe he was taking them to lose weight."

"How many people you know of take steroids to lose weight?" Terry asked.

"I don't know," Tank said. "Some of the guys on the football team take 'roids. I could ask them."

"Why don't you," Terry said.

"I will," Tank said.

The town beach in Cabot ran a couple of miles along the south end of town. It was broken occasionally by outcroppings of dark rock, rounded smooth by being so long beside the ocean. Terry sat with Abby on one of the outcroppings.

"That's where they found him," Abby said.

Terry nodded. The beach looked no different than it had before Jason washed up onto it.

"It doesn't look any different," Abby said.

"Nope."

"It should," Abby said. "You know?"

Terry nodded.

"He wanted to be a gardener," Terry said.

"I know," Abby said.

"So why would he be taking steroids?"

"I remember Tammy Singer offered him some grass once," Abby said. "He was, like, shocked."

"Yeah," Terry said. "He wouldn't drink. He didn't

smoke. He never got in trouble at school. And he's taking 'roids?"

"I think he was gay," Abby said.

"Yeah, probably," Terry said. "I know some gay guys are really into bodybuilding. But he wasn't. He didn't lift weights or anything. I don't believe it that he was taking them."

"You can't know that, Terry. There's lots you don't know about people. Everybody. You know? I mean Jason never said he was gay."

"But we all were pretty sure he was," Terry said.

"Yes."

"Well, he never said he was on 'roids either," Terry said. "But I'm pretty sure he wasn't."

"So what happened?"

"I don't know."

"There was a note," Abby said.

"Yeah."

"They found steroids in his system."

"Yeah."

"Maybe steroids do stuff we don't know about."

Terry was silent looking at the blank sand, where the waves washed in and hesitated and slid back leaving the tracings of foam behind them.

"We don't really know much about steroids, do we?" he said after a while.

"Not really," Abby said.

She was so pretty, he thought. And her dark hair always

smelled so nice when he was close to her, and she always listened to him and looked at him as if what he said, and what he was, were the most important things possible.

"Maybe it was a gay thing," Abby said.

"Taking steroids?"

"Yes."

"I never heard that," he said.

"Me either," Abby said. "You think maybe somebody did something to him?"

"I don't know."

"Maybe because he was gay," Abby said.

"Oh hell," Terry said. "Who around here cares about that anymore?"

"Some of the football players used to tease him."

"They tease everybody," Terry said.

"They don't tease you," Abby said.

"That's because they think I'm a boxer," Terry said.

"Well, you are."

"Not yet," Terry said.

"You do all that training."

"I'm learning," Terry said.

"I'd like to see you box sometime," Abby said.

"You can come to my next lesson, if you want."

"I'd love that," Abby said.

"Maybe George knows about steroids," Terry said.

CHAPTER 4

William Dawes Regional was a four-year high school. Grades nine through twelve were gathered, this Friday morning, in the assembly hall to hear about Jason Green's death. Mr. Bullard was at the podium. He was important. Not only was he the principal of the high school, he was also the superintendent of the district. To his right in a folding chair sat Mrs. Trent, the head of the Board of Selectmen.

"This past week," Mr. Bullard said, "one of our students, Jason Green, died tragically, an apparent suicide, induced by anabolic steroids. He was a fine student, and a fine boy. I'm sure many of you knew him. All of us mourn his loss. And all of us hope that his death will not be entirely in vain if it dissuades just one other young person from experimenting with a dangerous drug."

Mr. Bullard had very short graying hair. He was not so tall, but he was really wide. His suits never fit him right.

They were always tight around his chest and upper arms, and it made the lapels sort of stick out. Everybody knew he had played football. And everyone knew he lifted weights. He was often in the weight room at school. Terry knew Mr. Bullard could bench-press more than four hundred pounds.

"We know that this will trouble many of you," Mr. Bullard said. "We have, therefore, arranged that Mr. Helmsley and several other counselors will be available to you, here in the auditorium, starting this afternoon and continuing until there is no further need."

While Bullard was talking, Terry watched Mrs. Trent. She had on a gray suit, and pearls around her neck, and a knee-length skirt. She was sort of famous in town. Her picture was always in the paper with some politician. Looking straight at Mr. Bullard, she sat with her legs crossed and her hands folded quietly in her lap.

Not bad for an old broad, Terry thought.

"With the cooperation of Mrs. Trent, the chairman of the Cabot Board of Selectmen, those needing further counseling will be referred to an approved therapist at no expense to the student."

Terry leaned over and whispered to Abby. "I wonder how you get to be an *approved* therapist," he said.

Abby giggled and whispered to Terry. "You probably have to tell Mr. Bullard how big and strong he looks."

"The tragic death of a fine young man is always troublesome," Mr. Bullard said. "But the fact that the death may have been self-inflicted makes it even more troublesome. For each of us must ask himself, 'How did *I* fail him? What could *I* have done to help him?'"

Mr. Bullard's voice had that big empty sound that so many people had when they gave speeches, Terry thought.

The speeches went on for a while and then the students were dismissed for the day.

As they walked out of the auditorium, Abby said, "Were you looking at Mrs. Trent?"

"Yeah."

"She's too old for you," Abby said.

"I know," Terry said, "but she's got pretty nice legs."

"So do I," Abby said.

"How would I know," Terry said. "You wear jeans all the time, I never get to see them."

"Take my word," Abby said.

Terry grinned at her.

"For the moment," he said.

CHAPTER 5

When Terry brought Abby into the boxing room, George smiled at her and said, "Fight fan?"

"More a Terry fan," she said. "Is it okay if I watch?"

"Sure," George said.

He nodded at one of the two folding chairs in the room. Abby sat. Terry went through his warm-ups with the medicine ball, then taped his hands and held them out while George slid the big sixteen-ounce gloves onto them and tightened the Velcro closures.

"Okay, Novak," George said. "Let's see what you got."

They stood. Terry took his stance.

"We're going to shadowbox a little," George said to Abby. "Just let him get loose."

Abby smiled. George smiled back.

She's so amazing, Terry thought. *It's like she's not even a kid. Fifteen years old and charms everybody's butt off.*

"Two lefts and a right to the body," George said.

Terry did it.

"Two lefts to the head, right to the body," George said.

Terry did it.

"See how he keep his feet under him," George said. "Always got the left foot forward, always keep the spacing when he moving around?"

Abby nodded.

"Left to the body, right to the head," George said.

Terry did it.

"Keep it close in to the body," George said. "Turn your hip in. You're all torqued up after the left, let the right cross come out of that."

George showed him. It was always amazing to Terry how smooth and precise George's boxing moves were. And how awkward his own felt by comparison. George put on the punch mitts.

"Don't hit anybody with these," George said to Abby. "Just give him a chance to punch a moving target."

With the big padded mitts for targets, George moved around Terry, telling him combinations. Sometimes when Terry landed a good punch, it would make a satisfying pop.

"You hear that pop," George told Abby. "You know he land a good punch."

They moved around the small room, Terry's punches popping into the mitt.

"Now some bobbing," George said. "Stick with the left, bob under my punch, right to the body."

Terry jabbed George's left mitt with his own left, ducked under the half-circle sweep of George's left punch mitt, and turned a right hook into George's right mitt, held at body level.

"Again," George said.

They did it again. And again. Terry was breathing hard and he could feel the sweat soaking through his gray T-shirt.

"Okay," George said. "Left jab, bob, right to the head."

Terry did it. The jab slid off the edge of George's mitt. Terry stepped back in disgust.

"They can't all be winners," George said.

Terry nodded. He was very aware that Abby was in the room.

"Try it again," George said.

Terry tried it again and got two satisfying pops. He was breathing very hard.

"Again," George said.

Left jab. Bob. Right cross.

"Again."

Left jab. Bob. Right cross. Terry was gasping.

"Round's over," George said. "Take a seat."

Terry sat down next to Abby. She smiled at him.

"I didn't realize," she said, "how hard it is."

"Hard . . . for . . . me," Terry said.

"Hard for anybody," George said. "Bobbing and weaving take a lot of energy."

"It must be much harder if somebody is really trying to hit you," Abby said.

"Is," George said. "So you don't fight until you got all this grooved."

"But someday you have your first fight, if you're going to be a boxer," Abby said.

"You be scared," George said. "Everybody be scared. Once you got technique, fighting pretty much 'bout controlling fear."

"But . . . I mean that sounds right . . . but there you are and some man is running at you trying to hit you. How . . . ?"

"You keep your feet under you, you keep your stance, you try keep him off with your jab while you figure out what you gonna do. He charging at you and swinging wild, pretty soon he gonna open himself up, or he gonna run out of gas. That be your chance."

"Could you do that, Terry?" Abby said.

"I . . . don't . . . know."

"Not yet," George said. "I believe he got a cool enough head. But he ain't got enough training. Can't be thinking about it then. Got to be muscle memory. And you got to be able to trust it. Be a while 'fore we get there."

Terry's breathing had calmed.

"But we will," Terry said.

"Starting now," George said. "Ding ding. Round two."

CHAPTER 6

After his session, as he was doing his stretching, Terry said to George, "You ever take steroids?"

George shook his head.

"Used to pop a few NoDoz," George said.

"You know about steroids?" Terry said.

"'Nuff to know I don't want you messin' with them," George said.

"I won't," Terry said. "Can they make you crazy?"

"Don't really know," George said. "Hear a lotta talk about them, don't know how much is fact."

"You know anybody takes them?"

"Sure."

"Does it make any of them crazy?"

"Some of them already crazy," George said. "Why you want to know?"

"Kid I know committed suicide from taking steroids," Terry said.

"Oh," George said, "yeah. Read about that kid. You know him?"

"Yeah," Terry said. "And I don't think he was taking steroids."

George nodded and didn't say anything.

"Why would anyone take them?" Abby said. "If they're supposed to be so awful?"

George smiled.

"They may be," George said. "But everything you hear ain't for sure so."

"You mean you don't think they're bad?" Terry said.

"I mean I don't know," George said. "That the point. People say they bad, but you know lotta people take them, and they don't seem bad. Say you a fighter. Or a football player, or whatever, and you competing against people who take steroids? And it make them bigger and stronger and faster than you? And you keep losing your fights, or you gonna get cut from the football team? And fighting or football, or whatever, is all you know how to do?"

Terry nodded.

"Maybe you take the chance," Terry said.

"Maybe you do."

"You said you never took them," Abby said.

"Wasn't around so much when I was fighting," George said. "By the time they was popular, I didn't have no need for them."

"You think you would have taken them?" Abby said.

"I give you a pill that would make you stay beautiful and popular all your life," George said. "You take it?"

"She don't need it," Terry said.

"That's right, but do she know it?" George said.

Abby smiled.

My God, look at that! Terry thought.

"Do you think you might have a pill like that with you?" she said.

The three of them laughed.

"How old are you, girl?" George said.

"Fifteen," Abby said.

"Goin' on thirty-five," George said.

"You don't want me messing with 'roids," Terry said.

"'Cause you don't know," George said.

"I could look on the Internet," Terry said.

"Uh-huh," George said, "and you could stop people on the street and ask them."

"You don't trust the Web?"

"People get a chance to go on free and say anything they want to? Gonna get a lot of crap on there. 'Scuse me, Abby."

"Oh I say 'crap' all the time," Abby said.

George grinned at her.

"Hard not to," he said.

"So how do you find out about stuff like steroids?" Terry said.

"Medical folks, I guess," George said. "Don't know

much 'bout that. What I know is, until you know what you taking, and why, don't take it."

"I heard it could give you acne," Terry said, "and maybe stunt your growth, and maybe mess up your sex life."

"Uh-oh," Abby said.

Terry stared at her.

"What are you uh-ohing about?" he said. "We don't have a sex life."

"Yet," Abby said.

Terry's face felt a little hot, as if maybe he was blushing. The feeling that he might be blushing made him blush more.

"I guess I won't go there," he said.

Abby winked at George. And as they left, they could hear George chuckling to himself.

Wow, Terry thought. *Wow!*

CHAPTER 7

During free period, Terry went to the health center on the first floor of the high school. The woman at the reception desk had long gray hair and small round glasses with gold-colored frames.

"My name is Terry Novak," he said. "I'd like to see the nurse."

"You have a pass?"

"No ma'am, I'm just looking for information."

"Have to have a pass signed by a teacher or guidance counselor," the receptionist woman said, "to see the nurse."

"I'm not sick or anything," Terry said. "I just need to ask her about steroids."

"Not without a pass," the receptionist said. "School regulation."

"How 'bout if I got bitten by a rattlesnake," Terry said. "I still need a pass?"

"Don't get smart with me, young man," the reception-ist said.

"Wouldn't do much good," Terry murmured, mostly to himself.

"What did you say?"

"I said, yes ma'am, thank you ma'am."

"This is not an information booth, young man."

"I can see that," Terry said.

After the end of classes, Terry went down to the library and began to read in the newspaper files everything he could find about the death of Jason Green. He had left a note, probably typed and printed out on one of the computers in the school library. The note said simply that he was filled with ideas and feelings that he could no longer bear, and it was time to say good-bye. At the end of the note it said, "I love you all," and his name, typed, not written. He had been in the water for maybe a day, according to the coroner's office, and his system showed traces of steroids. As he read the accounts in the newspaper files, Terry realized suddenly that nobody at the coroner's office actually said the steroids caused his suicide. The newspaper stories all sounded as if that's what happened, and Mr. Bullard had sounded as if that was what happened, but the cops didn't actually say so, and neither did the medical examiner's office.

Tank lumbered into the library, saw Terry, and came over and sat down beside him.

"Whaddya doing?" he said, looking at the newspaper files.

"I'm reading about Jason."

"Man, you're really into that, aren't you?"

"I liked Jason."

"Yeah," Tank said. "He was okay. I think he was gay. You?"

"Yeah," Terry said. "I thought so."

"He ever say?"

"Not to me," Terry said.

"You didn't care?"

Terry shook his head.

"I didn't care," he said.

Tank nodded.

"Couple guys on the team are using steroids," he said.

"Football players?"

"Yeah. I won't tell their names," Tank said. "But they look good, and they told me it really helps."

"No bad symptoms?" Terry said.

"They say no."

"They know anything about Jason using them?" Terry said.

"Nope. They kind of laughed when I asked."

"Where do they get 'roids?" Terry said.

"They won't say. This is kind of hot stuff, Terry. Guys don't like to talk about it."

Terry nodded.

"You ever try them?" he said.

"Hell no," Tank said.

"I can see why," Terry said. "You get any bigger you'll have your own zip code."

Tank shrugged.

"What are you gonna do?" he said.

"I don't know," Terry said. "If you ever find out where the 'roids came from that your friends take . . ."

"If I can," Tank said. "Why do you want to know?"

"I don't know why I want to know," Terry said. "I don't know anything. I'm fishing."

"For what?" Tank said.

"Anything that bites, I guess. I can't seem to let go of it."

Tank laughed. The librarian glared at them from her desk in front.

"I known you all my life," Tank whispered. "You never let go of nothin'."

CHAPTER 8

I went on the Internet looking up steroids," Terry said.

"You learn anything?" Abby said.

"I learned that some people think they're poison, and some people think they're not."

They were hanging on the Wall together, across the common from the town library. There was no one else on the Wall. *I like being alone with her,* Terry thought.

"So we're nowhere," Abby said.

We!

"It's like you can't trust anything, you know?" Terry said. "You go to some anti-drug site and they preach to you about how bad it all is and talk like kids are morons and we don't know what the hell we're doing."

"No wonder we don't trust them," Abby said.

"Adults?"

"Yes," Abby said. "They're so know-it-all. And mostly they don't have a clue."

"Yeah."

"I mean why can't they say, you know, some people think steroids do this, and some people think they do that, and here are the known facts," Abby said. "Why isn't there anyplace like that to go to?"

"I don't know," Terry said.

Abby looked at him for a moment and smiled.

"And you don't care," she said.

Terry shrugged.

"Well," he said. "My mother's not much like that. She's pretty fair, you know. She doesn't pretend to know everything."

"And your father?" Abby said.

"He's dead," Terry said.

"I know. I'm sorry. I meant was he like your mom when he was alive?"

"He was okay," Terry said. "He just started teaching me how to box."

"What did he die of?" Abby said.

"Worked for the power company, got electrocuted on a job."

"Oh how awful," Abby said.

"Happened when I was twelve," Terry said. "I'm kind of used to it now."

"Your mother works," Abby said.

"Yeah. She's a bartender."

"Really?" Abby said. "Does she make enough? To live in this town?"

"Power company was to blame, I guess, when my father died," Terry said. "They gave her some money, and she paid off the mortgage and made some kind of trust fund for me to go to college. So yeah, we're getting by."

"Funny, I've known you since we were three," Abby said. "But I never knew how your father died."

"No reason you should. Hell, I don't know anything about your parents, what they do, what their names are. I don't know about anybody's parents."

"They do seem kind of, like, they don't have anything to do with this life."

"The one we have with each other?" Terry said.

"Yes, you and me, and the other kids. It's like adults don't get it that this life is going to school, hanging on the Wall," Abby said. "This is real life."

"You think a lot," Terry said.

"I guess so," Abby said. "Don't you?"

"Not so much," Terry said.

"You're thinking a lot about Jason Green," Abby said.

"That's different," Terry said.

"Why?"

"Because I want to find out what happened to him."

"So you think about problems and I think about how things are," Abby said.

"Actually," Terry said. "I think about you a lot too."

His father's wake was in the funeral home, Terry remembered. His mother and father weren't religious. He guessed he wasn't either. His father's casket was closed. The last time he had seen his father was when he'd put on his slicker and hard hat and left in a stormy night for a downed power line. Later there had been the phone call. And the rushing about in the night, and then everything became numb and he walked blankly through the rest of it, until here he was at the wake. He and his mother stood near the casket in the flat silence of the funeral parlor. There were some candles. His mother was very pale, he noticed. He wondered if he was. And all her movements seemed stiff. He felt kind of stiff too.

Friends of his mother and father came and went, saying awkward things about sorrow mostly to his mother. Some of the men shook his hand; some of the women patted him on the shoulder. There were no kids. Kids didn't go to wakes much. The people who worked in the funeral parlor were hovering around, guiding people to the guest book, looking sad. He hated them; they seemed phony to him. They didn't even know his father.

Then there was a kid, by himself, Jason Green, wearing a suit coat and tie. He walked past the funeral parlor man at the door, who looked at him as if he didn't belong, and came straight up to Terry.

"Hi," he said. "I wanted to tell you something."

Terry said, "Thanks for coming," as he had already said two dozen times. It was what his mother had told him to say. He too had on a coat and tie. It seemed odd to him.

"My father died when I was ten," Jason said. "After a while you won't feel so bad as you do now."

Terry nodded.

"You'll get used to it," Jason said.

Terry nodded again.

"I just wanted you to know," Jason said.

"Thank you," Terry said. "Thanks for coming."

CHAPTER 9

Seated behind his desk in his office, Mr. Bullard looked even bigger than when he was walking around. Mr. Bullard nodded Terry to a seat across from him and sat silently looking at him. He had his suit coat off and his sleeves rolled and his arms folded across his chest. His forearms were huge.

Like Popeye, Terry thought.

"You wanted to see me?" Terry said.

Bullard nodded silently. Terry waited.

"You went to the nurse yesterday," Bullard said after a time. "Without a slip."

Terry started to say yes sir, but stopped.

"Yes," he said.

"Do you know the school regulations?" Bullard said.

"Yes."

"Then you know that unauthorized visits to the school nurse are prohibited."

"I just wanted to ask her some questions," Terry said.

"About steroids," Bullard said.

"Yes."

"Why?"

"I'm just trying to figure out what happened to Jason," Terry said.

"Jason Green," Bullard said.

He remained motionless, sitting massively with his arms folded.

Trying to intimidate, Terry thought.

"Yes."

"And you are not happy with the official explanation?" Bullard said.

"I don't think Jason would take steroids," Terry said.

"There were traces in his system," Bullard said.

"But even if there were," Terry said, "would it make him crazy enough to kill himself?"

"Apparently," Bullard said.

Terry felt his stomach tighten. His throat felt tight. He took a deep breath and let it out slowly.

"I don't believe it," Terry said.

Bullard unfolded his arms and leaned forward in his chair and rested his thick hands on his desktop.

"You don't believe it," Bullard said.

"No."

"And you're an expert in these matters," Bullard said.

Keep your feet under you, Terry said to himself. *Keep your form.*

"I'm trying to learn," Terry said.

Bullard drummed softly on the desktop with his fingers. Terry waited.

Okay, keep your jab working, he thought. *Don't let him swarm you.*

"Mr. Novak," Bullard said.

Terry waited.

"Mr. Novak," Bullard said again. "How old are you?"

"Fifteen."

"Fifteen," Bullard said, and shook his head.

Terry was quiet. Bullard drummed his fingertips some more.

"I will not try to explain all of this to you," Bullard said after a time. "There is too much that you don't know. Let me just say this is an adult problem being tended to by adults. I do not want you to have anything further to do with it."

"I liked Jason," Terry said.

"We all liked him," Bullard said. "His death is tragic. And that is precisely why we do not wish to cause his mother more grief."

Terry didn't know what to say to that. He was quiet.

"I want you out of it," Bullard said. "Do you understand?"

Terry nodded.

"I understand what you want," Terry said.

Bullard slammed the palm of one hand on the desktop.

"And you'll do it," Bullard said. "You'll stop poking

your dumb fifteen-year-old nose into things you don't understand, or you'll have more trouble from me than you can imagine."

Jab, Terry thought. *Fight smart. Jab and cover.*

"Yes sir," he said.

Bullard pointed a thick forefinger at Terry.

"Behave yourself. I do not wish to have to take disciplinary steps."

"Yes sir," Terry said.

"You better believe it," Bullard said.

"Yes sir, I do," Terry said.

"All right," Bullard said. "Now get out of here."

"Yes sir," Terry said. "Thank you sir."

CHAPTER 10

I guess you were Jason Green's best friend," Terry said to Nancy Fortin. "Weren't you?"

She shrugged.

"Tell me about him," Terry said.

"You knew him," Nancy said. "What's to tell?"

Nancy was a square-built girl, strong looking, with short black hair. She was in the technical arts curriculum, where Jason had been.

"I didn't know him well," Terry said. "He seemed like a nice kid."

"He was. Lot of people dumped on him, though. He didn't play sports or anything."

"Lot of people thought he was gay," Terry said.

"You?"

"Yeah, I guess I thought so."

"But you didn't care."

"No."

"I don't know if he was gay or not," Nancy said. "He liked to draw and stuff. He was studying landscape design."

"He wanted to be a gardener, right?"

"Not a gardener," Nancy said. "A landscape designer. There's a difference."

"Oh," Terry said. "That why he's in the tech arts curriculum?"

"Yeah," Nancy said. "I guess. Why wouldn't he be?"

"Didn't seem the type," Terry said.

"We're not all stupid," Nancy said.

"I didn't say you were," Terry said. "I just figured Jason more for writing poetry and stuff."

"I guess you figured wrong," Nancy said.

"I do that a lot," Terry said. "What are you studying?"

"Culinary arts," Nancy said.

"Going to be a chef?"

Nancy nodded.

"Not a cook," she said.

Terry nodded.

"You think Jason killed himself?"

"I guess so," Nancy said. "Everybody says he did."

"But would he?" Terry said. "I mean you knew him really well. Would he kill himself?"

"How do I know?" Nancy said.

Nancy always had a tough sound in her voice, Terry thought, like she was mad about something.

"You were his best friend," Terry said.

She shrugged. Terry could tell she didn't like talking about this.

"His father's dead," Nancy said.

"I know," Terry said.

"His mother was kind of a problem."

"Why?"

"She got drunk all the time," Nancy said.

"Every day?" Terry said.

"After his father died," Nancy said. "Jason told me she would get drunk every night and pass out on the couch."

"That sucks," Terry said.

"Lot of things suck," Nancy said.

Terry decided not to ask about that.

"You think he was on steroids?"

"I don't know why he would be," Nancy said. "And, I mean I loved him, you know? But he sure didn't look like he was taking steroids."

Terry smiled.

"No he didn't," Terry said.

"He did take something for asthma," Nancy said. "I think he told me once it was some kind of steroid. We joked about it."

"He had asthma?"

"Sometimes," Nancy said. "The stuff he took seemed to help."

"And the gardening didn't bother it?"

"I told you before he was into landscape design," Nancy said.

"And he joked about taking steroids?"

"Yes, he thought it was funny, you know? How he wasn't into all that macho stuff," Nancy said. "But he was taking a steroid. . . . He didn't even like sports, or fighting, or weight lifting. He liked to draw."

"And now he's dead," Terry said.

"It's awful, isn't it?" Nancy said.

"Yes," Terry said. "It is."

CHAPTER 11

I throw my right at you," George said. "You block it with your left, counter with your right."

Terry did it.

"Or you block with your left," George said. "And counter with your left."

Terry did it, pounding the punches into George's big mitts.

"Keep your right up when you counter with your left."

Terry did it over. He kept his right hand high.

"Good," George said. "But what if I come straight in on you?"

He demonstrated with the big mitt.

"So I inside your left and you can't block me?" George said.

"I get . . . a big fat . . . lip," Terry said.

He was breathing very hard.

"You might," George said. "But if you check me, maybe you won't."

"Check," Terry said.

"It's a move they use a lot in martial arts," George said.

"I'm only . . . interested . . . in boxing," Terry said.

"Not so different," George said. "Get your hands up. We'll go through it slow motion. Stick your right hand at me, straight on."

Terry did, slowly. George diverted the punch slowly with his right hand, dropping his left at the same time.

"Just move the punch away. Not far. Just make him miss . . . and now, with your left you come up in a half circle and block him hard and get a nice shot at his head with your right. On the street you might use your elbow. It's right there handy."

They practiced a few times. Terry kept forgetting to drop his left when he checked with his right. His arms would tangle.

"Damn," Terry said.

"How many times you got to throw a punch," George said, "'fore it's part of the muscle memory?"

"Three, four thousand," Terry said.

"You done it seven times now," George said.

"Looks easier," Terry said, "when you do it."

"It is easier when I do it," George said. "I done it a million times."

Terry nodded. They worked some more on check-block.

And at the end of the session, Terry sat on the chair and George took off the gloves for him. Terry unwrapped his hands and caught his breath.

"How long we been doing this, George?" Terry said.

"Five months," George said.

"I'm nowhere near a boxer yet," Terry said.

George shrugged.

"And I don't want to get into a fight with anybody in the school yard or something," Terry said.

George nodded.

"But if I did, you know," Terry said, "I'd have a plan. I might win or I might not, but I would sort of know what I wanted to do."

"Good to have a plan," George said.

They were quiet as Terry unwrapped the self-sticking tape from his hands and wrists.

"It makes you feel, like, calm," Terry said.

"Calm is good," George said.

Terry balled the tape and dropped it into the wastebasket in the corner.

"You ever scared, George," Terry said, "when you were fighting?"

"Every fight," George said.

"The whole fight?"

"No," George said. "Once you get into the first round, you sort of lose the fear thing. First round you figure out if you got a legitimate chance to beat this dude or if you pretty much gonna concentrate on surviving."

"You didn't always think you'd win?"

George smiled.

"I could always hit," George said. "So I always had a chance, but you know pretty quick whether you as good as he is."

"How about a street fight? Not when you were a bouncer, but just, you know, some guy gives you grief, and you pop him?"

"You a professional fighter, Terry, you ain't supposed to be popping people on the street. Law give you trouble on that," George said. "Besides, most street fights be about proving something. You a fighter, you know what you can do. Ain't no need to prove it."

Terry nodded. His hands were unwrapped. His breath was back to normal. The sweat had dried. Still he stayed in the chair.

"You'd think it would be the other way," Terry said. "But it's like, the more you know about fighting, the less you fight."

"Maybe the less you be fighting about nothing," George said.

He put the big sixteen-ounce gloves onto the shelf and turned and looked at Terry for a moment. Terry thought he was going to say something, but he didn't. He just looked at Terry silently and nodded as if to himself.

"Don't be worrying 'bout the check-block thing," George said after a while. "You gonna get it."

SKYCAM IV

Gloria Trent stood on the front steps of the Cabot town hall. Her husband was beside her, and several others. A small group of reporters, including one television crew, was gathered in front of her.

"I have devoted my life to simple things," Gloria Trent said. "To my family, my husband, who is here with me today, and my daughter, who is now completing her freshman year at my own school, Taft University. I have also devoted myself, as my family responsibilities permitted, to public service, first as school committee chairperson of this lovely town, and then as the chair of the Cabot Board of Selectmen. Today, with my daughter away at school, I have more time available for my *second love, and with the enthusiastic support of my husband and daughter, I'm announcing my candidacy for the Republican nomination for governor of this great commonwealth."*

The people on the stairs with her applauded. Her husband raised both hands in the air as if he'd just won something. The news people took pictures.

"I will be in the primaries. I will be at the convention. I will preach the values I have lived by. Values all of us understand. The importance of family. The values of small town America. The importance of each individual to the community. We all matter. We all make a difference. I belong to no political machine. I will represent no special interest groups . . . except one. I will represent you, the people of this great commonwealth. My credentials are simple ones. I will govern honestly, with a sense of fairness and fundamental human decency, without which no governance can succeed in a democracy. It is a long road to walk. As we proceed, I will spell out the specifics of my position on every issue confronting us. For now let

me say only that I will walk that long road with my husband and my daughter, and I devoutly hope, with all of you. . . . Let us now begin."

Again the applause. Again the triumphant raising of hands by her husband.

When the applause had quieted, she located the television camera and gazed into it and said, "Questions?"

CHAPTER 12

The hero of William Dawes Regional High School left his cluster of assistant heroes and walked over to Terry in the high school weight room, where Terry was doing some light curls with fifteen-pound dumbbells.

"Novak," he said, "I wanna talk to you."

Terry continued to do his curls.

"Okay," Terry said.

The hero's name was Kip Carter. Thanks to him, William Dawes Regional had won the state championship in football three years in a row. He was a senior, two hundred pounds, blond hair, an all-state running back his junior and senior year. He was wearing a white tank top and black shorts over gray compression shorts. The tank top had ILLINI written on it in orange letters. It was a way of reminding everyone, Terry thought, that Kip Carter had a football scholarship to the University of Illinois.

"You are starting to get yourself in trouble, Novak," Kip Carter said.

Terry felt the little ripple in his stomach that he always felt when there was trouble. It wasn't fear, exactly. He didn't quite know what it was. But he didn't like it.

"Like what?" Terry said.

His face showed nothing. He kept curling the dumbbell.

"Like sticking your nose in where it doesn't belong," Kip Carter said.

He was three years older than Terry and fifty pounds heavier. He was very muscular. The veins showed across his biceps. Terry finished the curls and put the dumbbell down and sat on the bench with his forearms popping.

"Which is where?" Terry said.

He could feel the electric ripple again in his stomach.

"Snooping around asking about steroids," Kip Carter said. "Claiming, like, some people are taking them."

"I never claimed anybody was taking steroids," Terry said.

"You calling me a liar?"

Terry stood up.

"I never said anybody was taking steroids," Terry said.

"How come you're snooping around?"

"I'm trying to figure out what happened to Jason Green," Terry said.

"He killed himself," Kip Carter said. "Lotta fags commit suicide."

Terry put his hands up near his head in a kind of loose boxer's stance.

"What are you going to do, Novak? You gonna box me? You little creep," Kip Carter said.

Terry thought about what George said. Fighting about nothing. Kip Carter was nothing. What difference did it make what he said about Jason? What did Terry need to prove to Kip Carter? He'd keep doing what he was going to do. Wasn't that enough proof? It was. He dropped his hands, but he kept his feet under him.

"No," Terry said. "I'm not going to fight you."

"Damn straight," Kip Carter said. "Wouldn't be much of a damn fight anyway. You little turd."

"Sure," Terry said.

"You understand," Kip Carter said, "what I'm telling you? You forget about Jason Green and you forget about steroids, and you keep your nose clean. Maybe you make it to sophomore year without getting hurt."

"Sure," Terry said.

"Damn straight," Kip Carter said, and turned and walked out of the weight room.

He must like saying "damn straight," Terry thought.

CHAPTER 13

They were having coffee together in a shop on Main Street, across from the two-story brick building in downtown Cabot where Terry trained with George.

"Were you scared?" Abby said.

"I guess everybody's a little scared before a fight," Terry said.

"But there wasn't a fight," Abby said.

"I didn't know that," Terry said, "when I was being scared."

"Everybody's scared of Kip Carter All-American," Abby said. "Even Tank, I think."

Terry nodded.

"Would you fight with him if you had to?"

"I guess," Terry said.

"You can box," Abby said.

"I'm learning," Terry said.

"Maybe you'd win," Abby said.

"Maybe," Terry said.

He sipped his coffee. He didn't like it exactly. But he had decided he was too old now to be going out for sodas and frappes. He felt more like a serious guy drinking coffee. Abby had some too.

"Thing is," Terry said, "it's like George says. You learn how to box, you also learn how to not get in fights over nothing."

"And Kip Carter All-American is nothing?"

"Nothing to me," Terry said.

"Even though he says you can't do what you want to?"

"I'm going to do what I want to," Terry said.

"Try to find out what happened to Jason?"

"Yeah."

"What if he catches you and tries to beat you up?" Abby said.

"I'll try to make him stop," Terry said.

"What if he wins?"

"George says losing is part of fighting. Everybody loses. George lost eighteen times," he said. "Mohammed Ali lost once to Joe Frazier."

Abby was looking at him and frowning a little, the way she did when she was thinking about something. Terry believed it was the greatest look that was possible.

"If you gave it all you had when you won," Terry said. "And you gave it all you had when you lost. It's all anybody can ask you to do, George says."

"George, George, George," Abby said. "Do you believe everything George tells you?"

"I guess," Terry said. "The way George is, is a nice way to be."

"He doesn't seem all that successful," Abby said.

"I don't mean that," Terry said. "He seems like he's not scared of anything and he's not mad about anything and he's got nothing to prove to anybody, you know?"

Abby nodded.

"You're more like that than most kids," she said.

"Not like George," Terry said.

"It's too hard to be like George when you're a kid," Abby said. "I mean there's all the crap around you. Get good grades, get into college, be popular, do a bunch of extracurricular activities so the colleges will think you're well rounded. You're supposed to, you know, not have sex, not get drunk, not smoke dope, even though all the adults do it, and you have to listen to them always telling you about how these are the best days of your life."

Abby paused for breath.

"What crap," she said.

Terry smiled.

"Feel better?" he said.

"You know it's true."

"Yeah," he said, "I do."

"So how do you deal with it?" Abby said.

"I try not to pay so much attention to it," Terry said. "I just try to sort of keep going, do what I do. We'll grow up in a while."

Abby put her hand on top of his. He felt it throughout his whole self.

"I think maybe you already have," Abby said.

Terry felt as if the air were fresher than it had been and he could breathe deeper. It was as if the fresh air went into every part of him. He didn't know what to say. So he simply nodded. The waitress came down the counter and poured them more coffee. Terry put sugar and cream in his. Abby drank hers black. They both drank some coffee from the thick white diner-style mugs. Abby held hers in two hands.

"Who do you suppose told on you?" Abby said when she had put her cup down.

"Not that many kids knew I was interested in steroids," Terry said.

"Tank," Abby said. "And Suzi and Bev, we were talking by the Wall that day. You talked with Nancy Fortin."

"Yeah."

"Anybody else?"

"I don't think so," Terry said.

"Then it must have been one of them," Abby said.

"Why would they tell Kip Carter?" Terry said.

"To get in good with him," Abby said. "The question is: Why would he care?"

"Maybe he's juicing," Terry said. "And he's afraid he'll get caught."

"How are we going to find out?" Abby said.

Love that "we," Terry thought.

"I guess we'll have to ask," he said.

CHAPTER 14

They were hanging on the Wall.

"I never said anything to Carter," Tank said.

"You're sure?" Terry said. "Maybe when you were asking around about steroids?"

"I didn't ask," Tank said. "I just kinda looked and listened, you know."

"Is he one of the guys on 'roids?" Terry said.

Tank gave an elaborate shrug.

"Look at him," Tank said.

Terry nodded.

"And Nancy Fortin says she doesn't even know who Kip Carter is," he said.

"Everybody knows who he is," Tank said.

"Nancy's in her own world," Terry said.

"He was freakin' all-state," Tank said.

Terry shrugged. Abby came across the common from the library and joined them on the Wall. She held out a package of Altoid mints, which she liked and no one else could stand.

"Mint?" she said.

Terry shook his head.

"No thanks," Tank said. "Take the enamel off your teeth, I think."

Abby smiled at him.

"Sissy," she said.

"You talked to Suzi and Bev?" Terry said.

Abby popped a mint into her mouth. She nodded.

"Yes," she said. "Neither of them said anything to Kip Carter All-American."

"You believe them?" Terry said. "Maybe they wanted to score some points with the big man on campus?"

Abby laughed.

"Terry," she said, "most of the girls in school don't like Kip Carter All-American. He's always trying to cop a feel in the halls. You wear a loose top, he's always trying to get a peek down your front."

"Doesn't make him a bad person," Tank said.

"Oh Tank, oink!" Abby said. "Suzi's got no interest in him. He's creepy."

"How 'bout Bev?" Terry said.

"She says he's never spoken to her."

"Lotta people ain't spoken to Bev," Tank said.

"I know," Abby said. "Poor Bev, she's such a Goody‑Two-shoes."

"So how'd he know," Terry said. "If nobody told him, how'd he know."

They were quiet, sitting three in a row on the Wall. Abby was between the two boys, swinging her legs, and Terry liked how her jeans tightened over her thighs as she moved. He liked the strong smell of mint on her breath when she spoke.

"No kids told him," Abby said.

"That's what we're saying," Tank said.

"No," Terry said. "We're saying *nobody* told him."

"What's the difference?"

Terry looked at Abby.

"Some adults knew," Abby said.

"Bullard knew," Terry said.

"And the secretary in the nurse's office," Abby said.

Tank got it. He was excited. He wasn't used to getting things quickly.

"And the librarian," Tank said. "You was asking her about some steroid stuff, I remember."

"Why would they tell Kip Carter All-American?" Abby said.

"I don't know," Terry said.

"Maybe if we found out," Abby said, "we might know a lot."

There it is again, Terry thought, *"we"!*

CHAPTER 15

They were walking on the beach, which they liked to do. The weather was overcast, the wind was damp, and the surface of the ocean was gray and rough looking. There was something exciting about it, they thought. And if they dressed warmly, it was fun.

"You think it really was a grown-up that told Kip Carter All-American about you?" Abby said.

"Kids say they didn't," Terry said.

"But kids don't always admit stuff," Abby said.

"Neither do grown-ups," Terry said.

"True," Abby said. "So how are we going to find out?"

"Well," Terry said. "I suppose first thing is, we don't trust anybody."

"Except each other," Abby said.

"Except that," Terry said. "We don't know who's talking to who, or why. So we keep our mouths shut." He smiled. "Except if we're kissing."

"I'll keep that in mind when we start," Abby said.

"We will," Terry said, "sooner or later."

He always felt a little scared when he mentioned things like that to her. They were so good now, being best friends, it was as if he might spoil something.

"Probably," Abby said.

He hadn't spoiled it!

"And we only tell anything to each other," Terry said. Abby nodded.

"That won't help us find out anything," Abby said.

"I know."

They continued walking. Now it was raining a little. The beach was empty. It was one of the reasons they liked to walk in bad weather. They had it to themselves. Without saying anything, they had both chosen to walk away from the place where Jason Green's body had washed up. The wind had gotten stronger, and Abby took his arm and pressed against him as if for shelter. The harbor was getting rougher with the strengthening wind and the red channel buoys were tossing from side to side.

As they walked, he felt the pressure inside him. He always felt it when he was with Abby. He was thrilled to be with her. But he knew there had to be something more and he wasn't sure what would happen to them if they took the next step toward something more. What if the something more didn't work so well, and it meant they couldn't be friends anymore.

It would kill me, he thought.

"We could follow him," Terry said.

"Kip Carter All-American?"

"Yes."

"What would that prove?"

"If he spent a lot of time talking to the librarian or the secretary in the nurse's office or Mr. Bullard, maybe we'd know something."

"You don't think it's the librarian or the secretary," Abby said. "Do you?"

"No."

"You think it's Mr. Bullard."

Terry shrugged.

"Mr. Bullard also told me to stop messing around with this stuff," Terry said.

Abby nodded.

"And you think we'll catch Kip Carter All-American hanging out with Bullard?" she said. "What'll that do for us?"

"I don't know," Terry said. "I just don't know what else to do."

The wind was driving the rain at a small slant. Terry liked it. There was something exciting or romantic or *something* about rain.

"How about he's got his license and his father bought him a car and we can't even drive yet," Abby said. "How do we follow him if he drives?"

"We can follow him in school," Terry said.

"But what about after?"

"I guess all we can do is follow him where we can," Terry said.

Abby smiled.

"It's not much of a plan," she said.

"No," Terry said. "It isn't."

"But I suppose it's better than no plan," Abby said.

"Yes," Terry said. "It is."

The wind was strong now and the rain was hard. Terry felt as if all the energy of the storm was in the pit of his stomach, as if he might explode. She seemed so much calmer about their relationship. Sort of peaceful. Every time he joked about what might happen, like the kissing remark, she might joke or go along, but she always allowed him to think it might happen. That he and Abby might happen. That maybe they were happening already. He thought of his jokes as sort of momentary overflow. But he knew she knew. Sometimes he thought she knew everything.

She can't know everything. She's fifteen. And I'm fifteen.

He felt her arm through his and her shoulder against his and now and then their legs would brush as they walked together in the storm.

The hell with that, he thought. *We know what we need to.*

CHAPTER 16

Abby had two classes with Kip Carter All-American.

She watched him in those classes.

Terry had one class with Carter.

He watched him during that class.

They watched him in the corridors.

They watched him in the lunchroom.

They watched him during free periods when they could.

Sometimes they would be in the coffee shop at the same time.

They watched him there.

Sometimes Kip and other football players hung around after school near the football field and strutted, and pushed and shoved each other, and stared at girls. Some of the senior girls stared back. Some of them joined the group. When they did, there was a lot of talk and a lot of hard laughter.

They watched him flirt and swagger.

"Pretty raunchy," Abby said.

"Kind of gross," Terry said.

"It's not gross," Abby said. "It's . . ." She gestured with her hands as if she was searching for words. "They're just learning how to be men and women."

"They could do it quieter," Terry said.

He didn't like Abby hearing such talk, but he knew she wouldn't like it if he said that.

"Oh most of it is talk," Abby said. "Only a few of them actually do any of that stuff."

"How do you know?" Terry said.

"Girls talk about things," Abby said.

"How do you know they're learning to be men and women?"

"I think about stuff," Abby said.

"A lot," Terry said.

After Carter was through swaggering, and flirting, he walked home.

They followed him.

During the time they watched him, he never had any contact with the secretary in the nurse's office or with the school librarian. They saw him with Mr. Bullard three times.

"Doesn't mean there's anything," Terry said.

"But the math is good," Abby said. "He never saw those other people. He saw Bullard three times."

"'Course maybe Tank told him and won't admit it," Terry said.

Abby bumped her heels against the Wall, where they were sitting.

"We already said it's not much of a plan," she said. "But we also agreed it was the best one we had."

Mr. Bullard's tan Ford Fusion rolled slowly past the Wall and Mr. Bullard craned his thick neck to study the two of them sitting on the Wall. He always drove past the Wall on his way home after school.

"Gotta make sure nobody's smoking," Terry said.

"Or doing dope," Abby said.

"Or making out," Terry said.

"Probably hoping," Abby said.

"Bullard?"

"Yes. He's a pig, like Kip Carter All-American. He always looks at you when you walk past him in the hall. You know? Checks out your chest. Watches you as you walk away, looking at your butt."

"Bullard?"

"Uh-huh."

"He ever look at you?"

"Sure," Abby said. "What? Do you think I'm too homely?"

"No, no. God no. You're beautiful," Terry said.

Abby smiled.

"Why thank you, Terry," she said.

"But isn't Bullard married?"

"Uh-huh."

"And he's looking at high school girls?" Terry said.

"Uh-huh."

"Doesn't seem right," Terry said.

"Oh Terry," Abby said. "Sometimes you're like five years old."

"Well it doesn't," Terry said.

"It's just how men are," Abby said. "Men started staring at me the minute I started wearing a bra."

Her mention of her bra made him a little uncomfortable, but he didn't want her to know that.

"Grown men?"

"Sure, any girl knows that. It doesn't mean anything. It's just how it is."

The tan Fusion moved on.

"Couldn't catch us doing anything," Abby said.

"Probably ruined his day," Terry said.

They sat quietly.

"You know what I think," Terry said after a time. "I think we ought to follow Bullard."

"Mr. Bullard?"

"Uh-huh," Terry said. "Let's decide it's him and see what we can find out about him."

"What if he catches us?"

"We'll have to be sure he doesn't," Terry said.

Abby nodded slowly.

"Be kind of fun, wouldn't it," she said.

Terry nodded. Neither of them said anything for a time. Abby bumped her heels some more against the Wall.

"I didn't mean you're really like five years old," Abby said. "Actually most of the time you seem like a grown man to me. You just don't know so much about sex."

"I can learn," Terry said.

Abby looked straight at him and her smile was wide and bright.

"I'll bet you can," Abby said.

SKYCAM V

He was a drug salesman for one of the big drug companies, and once a week he called on doctors at Mass General Hospital. When he was through for the morning, he would get a gym bag from his car in the parking garage and go to the cafeteria. There he would meet a big man who had a similar gym bag. They would have coffee together, and when they left, each would take the other's gym bag.

The cafeteria was called Eat Street, and whenever he went there, the salesman always smiled to himself. The place was so cutesy. The man he met was definitely not cutesy. He reminded the salesman of a rhinoceros: squat and thick and dangerous. The salesman was a little afraid of him, but when he took the big man's gym bag back to his car and opened it in the parking garage, the money was always there, in cash.

The salesman wondered sometimes what he'd do if there was no cash in the gym bag, if the big man stiffed him. He wouldn't dare confront him. And even if he did, he couldn't confront him in Eat Street. He didn't even know the big man's name, or where he was from, or even what he did. All he knew was the cash in the gym bag every week when they swapped.

If the big man ever stiffed him, he guessed he'd have to eat the cost of that week's delivery and not make another one. On the other hand, he wouldn't be making any more deliveries, and the big man didn't know his name either. The salesman could park in a different place and not come to Eat Street, and the whole thing would be over. He'd miss the money, but there were other people he could make an arrangement with, if he needed to. But cross that bridge when he came to it. Right now, he was getting his money. And the big ugly rhino was getting his steroids.

Fair all around.

CHAPTER 17

Terry was taping his hands.

"I never see fighters using this check-block thing," Terry said. "I watch those classic fight films a lot."

"They use the check part," George said. "Foreman used it. But they do it so quick and easy that you don't much notice."

"What about the block part?"

"Mostly martial arts," George said. "I just threw it in, case you liked it."

"I want to box," Terry said.

George nodded.

"Martial arts guys do a lot of things with that check-block move," he said. "Don't do you no harm to know it."

Terry put his hands out and George slipped the big gloves on and Velcroed them tight.

"Okay," George said. "Today combinations. I'm going to move the mitts around. You do left jab, right to the body, left hook, right uppercut, right to the head depending on how I move the gloves. We'll do it slow motion to start."

They walked through the sequence.

"You got it," George said. "Now, here we go."

George put the left mitt up. Terry jabbed it. George turned the right mitt over. Terry gave it an uppercut. They moved slowly, George shuffling left or right, Terry following.

"Keep your stance," George said. "Set up after you punch. Be quick, but don't hurry."

The punches made a satisfying pop when they landed solid in the mitts. As Terry got tired, the punches began to slide off with less pop.

"Torque your forearms," George said. "First two knuckles . . . Breathe . . . Keep your feet under you . . . Left foot forward . . . Punch from the floor . . . Turn your hip into it . . . Good, take a seat."

Terry went and sat. He was sweating. His chest was heaving. He felt good.

"How'd you come to be a fighter, George?" Terry said.

George smiled. Terry noticed he was not trying to catch his breath.

Hell, Terry thought, *I was doing all the punching.*

"Old story," George said. "Grew up in Baltimore. No father. Mother working two jobs to keep us going. I spent most of my time in the streets. In that part of Baltimore, on the streets, you had to fight. Didn't have no choice. Got in some trouble. So my mother say you gonna fight anyway, maybe you should learn how. Maybe make some money. Took me to a priest, white priest, run an athletic program for street kids. Got me signed up for boxing."

"You Catholic?"

"Nope," George said. "Wasn't white neither. Priest didn't care. Went to Golden Gloves and then pro. Made a living. Most of the kids I fought in the street with are dead or in jail."

"Wow," Terry said. "A real priest."

George smiled and nodded.

"Yep," George said. "A real one."

They went another round on the combinations and moving. Then they did what George called speed drills.

"Want you hit that heavy bag, left-right, left-right, fast as you can, keepin' your form. Gonna do it for a minute."

Terry did it. George counted it down.

"Good," George said. "Take a break."

Terry went, and sat, and breathed.

When he could, he said, "I used to think, like, a priest wouldn't do a bad thing. A teacher wouldn't do that, you know?"

"Uh-huh."

"But sometimes they do bad things. Priests can be bad. Teachers, you think they're all supposed to be good, and some of them aren't."

"Way it is," George said.

"Makes it hard to trust people," Terry said.

"It do," George said.

CHAPTER 18

They were hanging on the Wall: Terry and Abby, Tank, Suzi, and a small smart kid named Otis. A silver BMW sedan pulled up in front of them and Kip Carter got out with two friends.

Otis said, "Uh-oh."

"Hey, boxer boy," Carter said. "You keeping your nose clean?"

Terry didn't say anything.

"What do you want?" Abby said.

"Want to know if boxer boy's being good," Carter said.

"Why don't you go bother somebody else?" Abby said. "Creep."

"'Cause we want to bother you, slut," Carter said.

"Hey," Terry said. "Watch your mouth."

"He's telling me to watch my mouth," Carter said to one of his friends.

The friend's name was Gordon. He played linebacker and was part of Carter's entourage.

"Or you'll do what," Gordon said.

"I told him about you being a boxer," Carter said. "And Gordon don't think much of that. Gordon thinks he can kick your butt."

Terry nodded slowly.

"I think he can too," Carter said. "You think so, Mikey?"

Mikey was another hanger-on. He played center on the football team and followed Carter around most of the rest of the time.

"Sure he can," Mikey said.

"How 'bout you, dweeb," Carter said to Otis. "What do you think?"

"I don't know," Otis said.

"And you, Kitty Cat?" Carter said to Abby. "What do you think?"

"I think you should buzz off," Abby said.

"Me too," Suzi said.

"Well we've heard from the Kitty Cats," Carter said to Terry, "what you think."

Terry took in a long breath of air, and slid off the wall.

"Terry," Abby said. "Don't."

"Hey, the boxer boy's gonna show us his stuff," Carter said. "You stay out of this, Tank."

"You too," Tank said.

Carter laughed.

"Sure, sure," he said. "I'm thinking Gordon won't need no help."

Terry went into his stance. Left foot forward. Hands high. He heard Carter laugh. It wasn't about Carter now. It was about him and Gordon. They circled each other. Gordon seemed a little stiff in his movements, Terry thought. Maybe he's a little scared too. Gordon lunged at him. Terry put a left jab onto his nose. It stopped Gordon. Terry followed with a straight right, again on the nose, torquing his forearm, turning his hip in, keeping his feet under him, breathing out hard when he threw the punch. Gordon yelped. The blood spurted from Gordon's nose. Gordon put his hands to his nose, and Terry landed a heavy left hook on his cheekbone and Gordon fell down.

"My nose," Gordon said. "He broke my damn nose."

Abby took a packet of Kleenex from her bag, and jumped down from the wall, and gave the Kleenex to Gordon.

Terry turned, still in his stance, toward Carter. Tank slid off the wall and stood beside Terry. Then Otis jumped down and stood with Tank. Carter looked at them and didn't say anything. Gordon took some of the Kleenex in a wad and held it against his nose.

"I think it's broke," he mumbled.

"Why don't you get Gordon into your stupid car," Abby said to Carter, "and take him to the doctor?"

Carter nodded.

"Get him in the backseat," Carter said to Mikey.

Mikey helped Gordon up and they got in the car.

"Careful with the blood," Carter said.

He looked silently at Terry for a moment.

"Don't change nothing," he said. "What I told you in the weight room."

Terry kept his stance.

"And keep in mind . . . I ain't Gordon," Carter said, and turned and walked around and got in the driver's seat and drove his silver BMW away.

Terry let his arms drop. The fight had lasted about ten seconds, but he was breathing heavily. His hands hurt where he had punched Gordon. No gloves. No tape. Lucky he didn't break something. He felt his hands. They seemed intact.

"Man, that was fast," Otis said.

"You okay?" Abby said.

"Yeah, sure. He didn't even hit me."

"I think you did break his nose," Tank said.

Terry nodded. He was exhausted. *How do you get exhausted in a ten-second fight?*

"This will be all over school tomorrow," Suzi said.

Abby was looking at Terry. He looked back at her.

"I'll bet they won't bother Terry anymore," Otis said.

Terry shrugged. He felt a little shaky. He'd have to talk with George about this. He hadn't thought about how he'd feel after a fight.

"Terry," Abby said. "Can we take a walk? Just you and me?"

"Sure," he said.

His left hand was beginning to throb a little where his left hook had landed on Gordon's cheekbone. When he got home, he'd put ice on it.

As they walked away, Abby took his hand.

First time!

Behind him he heard Otis say, "I'm serious, maybe I should learn to box."

"I don't know, Otis," Suzi said. "Maybe you're better to out-think them."

"How do you feel?" Abby said.

"I'm fine," he said.

"No," Abby said. "You're not."

"How do you know?"

"I can tell," Abby said. "I know you."

He liked it that she cared how he was. He liked it that she knew him well enough to tell when he wasn't all right.

"I'm a little shaky," he said.

"A fight like that must give awfully intense feelings," Abby said.

"I guess," Terry said.

"Feelings like that take a lot out of you."

"Sometimes," he said.

"And sometimes not?" she said.

He looked at her without speaking for a while.

"And sometimes not," he said.

It was Abby's turn to be silent for a time.

Finally she said, "Are we still talking about the fight?"

"I don't think so," Terry said.

CHAPTER 19

The problem with following Bullard," Abby said while she waited for her coffee to cool, "is even worse than Kip Carter All-American. Bullard drives everywhere."

"I thought of that," Terry said. "I say we need a spotter network."

His left hand was swollen and sore.

"A what?"

"We know kids who live all over town. Everybody got a cell phone, practically. You know, Otis lives in East Cabot, you live near the Center, Nancy Fortin lives by the park. We get people all over town to keep an eye out for Mr. Bullard. Keep track of where he goes, what he does."

"And they could report to us by cell phone," Abby said.

"I don't have a cell," Terry said.

"Why don't you get one already?"

Terry shrugged.

"We don't have much extra money," he said.

"Doesn't matter," Abby said. "I got a cell. They can report to me."

"We have to use people we can trust," Terry said. "We can't let Bullard know, or Kip Carter and his crew either."

"I'll do it," Abby said. "I got a lot of girlfriends who'd love to do this. Let me organize this. We'll like chart his movements."

Terry looked at her and laughed.

"Abby Hall," he said. "Girl detective."

She grinned at him. Her eyes were very big. Her mouth was wide. When she smiled, it made her face seem bright, and he always thought of her smiling like that. It made him think of *glee* when she grinned like that, as if something wildly exciting was about to happen.

"Well," she said, "it is kind of fun, isn't it?"

"Not if Kip Carter pounds me into a fish cake," Terry said.

"Maybe he can't," Abby said. "Gordon couldn't."

"Gordon is not Kip Carter," Terry said.

"Don't you think if Kip Carter All-American thought he could pound you into a fish cake he'd have done it instead of siccing Gordon on you?"

Terry shrugged.

They were in the Coffee Café in the center of town. The café had not set out to be a high school hangout. But it was downtown, next to the cinema, four blocks from the high school, and never seemed crowded in the afternoon. Slowly the kids started hanging out there, and the more they hung out there, the more adults didn't come, so that finally the place had become a high school hangout. Whether the owners liked it or not, it was a fact. If you were a high school kid, the café was where you went.

"Have you found out any more about steroids?" Abby said.

"I've been on the Internet, but there's, like, too much information and they say different stuff, and I don't know what's true and what's not."

"And there's no one to ask?" Abby said.

"Like who? My mother? She's a bartender. She doesn't know any more than I do about steroids."

"And there's no one else," Abby said.

"Nobody that knows anything. I mean I can't just make an appointment with some doctor and say, 'tell me about 'roids.' You know?"

"I do," Abby said. "I've been thinking about that."

"You do a lot of thinking," Terry said.

"Yes I do," Abby said, and smiled the big smile at him again. "I'm very smart."

"Modest too," Terry said.

"Absolutely," Abby said.

"So what have you been thinking?"

"Gary," she said. "At the drugstore."

"Sarkis Pharmacy?"

"Yes," Abby said. "He's very nice, and he must know about steroids. I bet he's got a book or something."

Terry nodded, looking at her.

She is smart, he thought, *and the best part is, she's being smart for me.*

"Let's go over there now," Terry said.

"On the hunt," Abby said.

And they left.

You roughed him up a little?" the big man said.

"Sort of," the jock said.

"But you didn't touch him," the big man said. "Right? You had somebody else do it."

"I had Gordo do it."

"And?" the big man said.

"Novak broke Gordo's nose."

The big man sat back in his chair behind his desk and shook his head.

"Never send a boy . . ." he said.

"Gordo's my age," the jock said.

The big man shook his head.

"It's a saying," the big man said.

"Yes sir," the jock said.

"So, I guess you didn't send a good message."
"He got him with a lucky punch," the jock said.
"Kid's a ninth grader."

"Do you think it will make him back off?" the big man said. The jock shook his head.

"I shoulda done it myself," the jock said. "If you hadn't told me not to, I'da kicked his butt."

"No," the big man said. "You don't touch him. You get in trouble and they tie you to me . . . You keep your hands to yourself."

"Maybe we scared him enough anyway," the jock said.

"I'll bet," the big man said. "Keep an eye on him just in case he isn't terrified."

"He's nothing," the jock said. "He got a lucky shot in on Gordo is all. You give me the go-ahead, I'll clean his damn clock."

"Do not swear in this office," the big man said. "This isn't about who can win a fight with who. You don't think he could get a lucky shot in on you?"

"No sir, I can take him easy. He's a punk."

The big man nodded.

"You do what I tell you," the big man said. "You watch and you wait and you report back to me. I don't want you laying a hand on him. We need to ratchet up the pressure, we'll do it when I say so."

The jock nodded.

"You want to play Big Ten football?" the big man said.

"Yes sir."

"Name in the paper, a hundred thousand fans every Saturday? Pro scouts?"

"Yes sir!"

"Then do what I tell you and make sure you don't tarnish this office."

"Yes sir."

"You been seeing the nurse regularly?" the big man said.

"Just like you told me," the jock said.

"Good," the big man said. "You keep doing

what I tell you, and everything will be smooth as new ice. Okay?"

"Okay," the jock said.

"Okay, what?" the big man said.

"Okay, sir?"

"Thank you," the big man said.

CHAPTER 20

At the drugstore, Gary Sarkis gave them ten photo-copied pages of a medical update about steroids from a big HMO.

"Lotta medical language," he told them. "But you can wade through it. You need help, call me."

"Do you take steroids for asthma?" Terry said.

"Of a sort," Gary Sarkis said. "In very small amounts. But it's not the same stuff that athletes use."

They took the pages to the Wall and sat and began to read them. Terry would read a page and hand it to Abby. When Abby read it, she underlined things in yellow.

When they had both finished, Terry said, "Yikes."

"It does take some wading," Abby said.

"You get anything out of it?" Terry said.

Abby giggled.

"If you take some of these things, your . . . testicles might shrink," Abby said.

"Come on," Terry said.

"Says so right here," Abby said, and marked the passage.

Terry read it again.

"'Testicular size may decrease if androgen is taken for many years,'" he said. "I missed that first time through."

Abby giggled again.

"I didn't," she said.

"So *androgen* is another word for *steroid*," Terry said.

"I think so."

"So here's the psychological effects," Terry said. "That's what we want."

"It doesn't say anything about suicide," Abby said. "'Major mood disorders and aggressive behavior' is what it says."

"Suicide is a *major* mood disorder," Terry said.

"But if they meant suicide, they'd say so, wouldn't they?"

"I guess. Jason certainly wasn't aggressive." He pointed. "What's this mean, you think?"

Abby read aloud.

"'Most psychological descriptions are uncontrolled.'"

"Uncontrolled how?" Terry said.

"Like the studies aren't, um, careful, you know?" Abby said. "They're more just what people say about steroids. The doctors are, like, not sure if it's true. A lot of this stuff is like that."

"Well, hell," Terry said. "Who's going to tell their doctor they're on 'roids?"

"I guess that's the problem," Abby said.

They read the pages again.

"Lot of stuff they think might happen to you from juicing," Terry said.

"And over here it says they're not all that sure that it does you much good."

Terry nodded.

"Look at this," he said. "If women take it."

Abby looked down and read where he pointed.

"Oh wow," she said. "Acne, facial hair . . ."

"Sounds great, doesn't it?" Terry said.

"Can't wait to try it," Abby said.

"All of this stuff is written about jocks," Terry said. "Doesn't talk about ordinary kids like Jason."

"Maybe because ordinary kids like Jason don't take steroids," Abby said.

"Nothing here makes me think he did," Terry said.

"No," Abby said. "Sounds more like Kip Carter All-American to me."

"Yeah," Terry said. "Maybe you should date him."

"Me?" Abby said.

Terry gave her a straight-faced serious look.

"Give you a chance to find out if anything's shrinking," he said.

"Oh ugh!" Abby said.

And they both began to giggle.

CHAPTER 21

Geoorge was wrapping Terry's hands.

"Little swollen," George said.

"I had a fight."

"How'd you do?" George said.

"I broke the guy's nose," Terry said.

"So you won?"

"Yeah."

"Better than losing," George said. "Why'd you fight?"

"Other guy started it," Terry said.

"How?"

"Was gonna beat me up," Terry said.

"Front of other people?"

"Yes."

"You know why?"

"I think it's about that kid, Jason, who died a while ago?"

"The one you been wondering about," George said.

"Yeah."

"Why somebody want to beat you up 'bout that?" George said.

"I don't know."

"You looking into it?" George said.

"Yes."

"Maybe they want you to stop," George said.

Terry shrugged. George looked at him for a moment. He looked like he wanted to say something. But he didn't.

"What?" Terry said.

George shook his head and finished wrapping Terry's hands.

"You gonna tell me mind my own business?" Terry said. "'Cause I'm a kid, and I don't know what I'm doing?"

"Nope."

"You were gonna say something," Terry said. "What?"

George slid the gloves onto Terry's hands and cinched the Velcro closers shut.

"I was gonna tell you to be careful," George said.

"I can take care of myself," Terry said.

"Mostly," George said. "Nobody can do it always."

"So I just quit and go hide?"

"Nope."

"So," Terry said. "What?"

"So, nothing, that's why I didn't say it."

They looked at each other.

"I don't get it," Terry said.

George nodded.

"Kid mattered to you," George said.

"I felt sorry for him," Terry said. "Got no father. Mother's a drunk. Everybody thinks he's a fag."

"You?" George said.

"Yeah, I guess he was."

"You don't care."

"No," Terry said. "Got nothing to do with me."

"You not gay," George said.

"No," Terry said. "You care?"

"No," George said. "I don't care. But that little girl might be awful disappointed."

Terry smiled.

"I hope so," he said.

"You doing what you think is the right thing to do," George said. "Maybe be some risk. Smart to be careful. Don't want to hide all your life. If you gonna face up to it, might as well start now."

"You saying I should go ahead?"

"Yep."

Terry didn't know what to say.

"So this guy comes at you," George said, "swinging, and you hold him off with your jab."

"Yeah."

"And he tries a big John Wayne roundhouse punch," George said.

"Yeah."

"And you block it with your left?"

"And hit him with my right, straight on."

"Broke his nose."

"Yes."

George smiled.

"Fight over," he said.

"Uh-huh."

George smiled more.

"Just remember," he said. "You fight somebody knows a little something, won't be so easy."

"Thanks, George," Terry said.

"For what? Teaching you left block, right punch?"

"Including that," Terry said.

George picked up the big round punching mitts.

"Come on," he said. "You gonna be street fighting, may have to teach you some other things."

"You've already taught me a lot," Terry said.

"You learned a lot," George said. "Which ain't always the same thing."

CHAPTER 22

They were on the rocks at the beach, in their place, on the point of an outcropping where the waves broke beneath them and left lacy patterns of foam on the surface of the water. Abby had her big notebook on her lap.

"I've been organizing," she said.

"I bet you have," Terry said.

"I got Otis," she said. "Tank, Nancy Fortin, a friend of Jason's that Nancy got, Perry Fisher."

"Don't know him," Terry said.

"Me either," Abby said. "But Nancy says he wants in. I got Bev and Suzi. Steve Bellino says he'll help."

"Bellino?" Terry said. "He's a really good ballplayer."

"I know," Abby said. "I think he hates Kip Carter All-American."

"Not a bad thing," Terry said.

"And I think he's going to get some other guys," Abby said. "Maybe Mitchell, maybe Carly Clark."

"Carly Clark?"

"The basketball player," Abby said. "The guy who just transferred in."

"I know who he is," Terry said.

"So we already got a pretty good spy system set up."

"Thanks to you," Terry said.

"Can I be known as the Spymaster," Abby said, deepening her voice as much as she could.

"You bet," Terry said. "Think they'll keep quiet about this?"

"I think so," Abby said. "They all hate Bullard, and they all hate Kip Carter All-American, and I think this is their chance to do one or both of them some damage."

"Any of them doing it for Jason?" Terry said.

"Nancy, probably," Abby said. "Probably Perry Fisher. The rest of us are doing it for you."

"You too?"

"Of course, me too," Abby said. "I'll do anything you want to do, you know that."

"Anything?" Terry said.

"Except that," Abby said. "Yet."

"Yet," Terry said.

"Yet," Abby said.

"What are we waiting for?" Terry said.

"I don't know," Abby said. "It just seems too soon."

Terry was quiet for a moment and then he nodded.

"I think so too," he said.

"Do you know why?" Abby said.

"No. You?"

"No," Abby said.

Terry shook his head. They were quiet, watching the foam patterns slide backward out of the inlets in the rock. It was the first time they'd ever spoken seriously about it. It made him nervous. Kind of exciting, though!

"They going to, ah, report in to you?" Terry said after a time.

"Yes," Abby said, "and I'll write it down and try to like find a pattern or something. And we'll talk."

Terry smiled at her.

"Will we ever," he said.

CHAPTER 23

Terry saw Gordon in the corridor between classes. Gordon was wearing sunglasses, which didn't fully succeed in covering his two black eyes. His cheeks were puffy too. Gordon either didn't see him or pretended not to. In the cafeteria, Kip Carter looked right through Terry. When he went to English class, he saw Mr. Bullard standing by the door.

"I want to talk with you," he said.

Terry stopped and waited. Mr. Bullard took his arm and steered him away from the door and into a stairwell.

"You are getting a pretty bad reputation around here," Bullard said.

Terry nodded.

"I understand you got into a fight," Bullard said.

"Not at school," Terry said.

"Don't give me any smart mouth," Bullard said. "You got into a fight."

"Yes sir," Terry said.

"You start it?"

"No sir."

"I heard you did," Bullard said.

"No sir," Terry said.

"What's your story?" Bullard said.

"Gordy wanted to see if I could box," Terry said.

"And you broke his nose?"

"Yes sir."

"He says you sucker punched him," Bullard said.

"He swung on me," Terry said. "I blocked it and countered."

"Kip Carter supports Gordon's story," Bullard said. "You think he's lying."

"Yes sir."

"Well," Bullard said. "I don't think so. And I've already given this as much time as I'm going to. The next time you step out of line, you're suspended. You understand that?"

"Even if it's not my fault?" Terry said.

"You're a troublemaker, Novak. You'll keep your nose clean or I'll lower the boom on you."

Hulking before him, Mr. Bullard reminded Terry of some kind of animal. A rhino, maybe. Thick and short and massive and ugly and mean. His eyes were kind of small, and they looked even smaller because his face was so wide. Made him look sort of dumb. Terry smiled to himself for a moment. *Maybe he is dumb,* Terry thought.

Bullard saw the smile.

"There's nothing funny going on here," Bullard said.

There's a lot funny going on here, Terry thought. But he kept his face blank. There was no point taking Bullard on direct. *What was it George said? Something about deciding early in the fight whether it was one you could win or one where you mainly tried to avoid getting hurt.* He knew that this was that kind of a fight. He wasn't going to win, right now, at least. And he wasn't going to win alone. But on the other hand, the fight wasn't over. And every day he seemed a little less alone. *Pick your spot,* he said to himself. *Pick your spot.* Right now he knew that he was in a position to get kicked out of school anytime Bullard wanted to. He got kicked out, he got kicked out. He wasn't going to stop. He was in too deep. It wasn't even about Jason anymore. Something bad was going on, and he wasn't going to be chased off by a pig like Bullard until he found out what it was.

Things were developing.

CHAPTER 24

Abby was sitting in a booth in the Coffee Café with her legs tucked under her. There was a book bag open in the seat beside her, a green manila folder open on the tabletop. She had a ballpoint in her hand and was drinking coffee with the same hand and talking on her cell phone. She grinned at Terry as he slid in across from her. She put the coffee down and wrote in her green folder and nodded and wrote some more.

"Okay," she said. "Thanks, Otis."

She broke the connection and looked at Terry.

"AIA headquarters," she said.

"AIA?"

"Abby's Intelligence Agency," she said.

Marcia the waitress brought Terry some coffee and freshened up Abby's.

When they were alone, Terry reached across and took the green folder and pulled it to him and turned it around so he could read it.

"What have you got?" he said.

"My spy log," Abby said.

"Who are all these people? No names? Just numbers?"

"Some of my friends," Abby said. "Some friends of my friends. Some friends of their friends. Lots of people are in on this. I give them each a number. I'm the only one who knows what number is who. They like it. It's fun."

"They could get in trouble," Terry said.

"Half the school?" Abby said. "And for what? We're just keeping track of people. What's wrong with that?"

"Bullard wouldn't like it," Terry said.

Abby grinned.

"I think that's why a lot of kids are doing it," she said.

"And if Bullard catches you?" Terry said. "What will you do?"

Abby smiled widely and stuck out her tongue.

"That's what you'll do?" Terry said.

"Uh-huh."

Terry stared at the list of numbered entries in the folder.

"Well," he said. "At least we got him surrounded."

"Yes," Abby said. "What I did was, I gave all these people my cell phone number, and whenever they see either Mr. Bullard or Kip Carter All-American, they call in and tell me about it. A lot of time they leave it on my voice mail and I, you know, compile it in my room, after supper."

"And you keep track of it all?"

"On this chart," Abby said.

She took a piece of lavender-lined white paper out of the folder and held it up for him. He took it and they leaned toward each other across the table as she explained it. The top of her head touched his. Her hair smelled of shampoo.

"See," she said. "I do one for Bullard and one for Kip Carter All-American. Everyone they saw. Everywhere they went. Everything they did. And the date and time."

"How about when no one saw them?" Terry said. "Like if Bullard went to some meeting in Boston or something."

"That time is left blank," Abby said. "Sometimes we find out later and we fill it in. After a while we'll get a pretty good idea of what they do all day, you know?"

"Kip Carter too?" Terry said.

"Yes." She held up another sheet of paper. "Same thing for him."

"Lot of work," Terry said.

"You can help me. We'll sit down at the end of the week and see if we see a pattern. Like we're detectives."

"Abby Hall," Terry said. "Girl Detective."

"And her trusted companion," Abby said. "The Boxer!"

Terry put his hands up in his boxing stance for a moment.

They both laughed.

"You know," Terry said. "We really are going to find out what happened to Jason Green."

"Yes," Abby said. "We really are."

CHAPTER 25

Abby sat at her desk in front of the window in her upstairs bedroom. The messages started in the morning.

"Hi, Abb, it's number seventeen," a girl's voice said.

That would be Suzi.

"Mr. Bullard drove by a minute ago while I was waiting for the bus. . . . I assume he's going to school like the rest of us poor convicts. . . . Why doesn't the cheap creep get a real car. . . . He looks so funny all squeezed into that little sardine can he drives. . . ."

"Hi, Abby, it's Otis, I forgot my number . . . anyway I saw Bullard at that place, near me, where the tech arts kids are building a house. . . . Kip Carter was there too."

"It's number eleven," a boy's voice said.

Abby checked her list. Number eleven was Jason's friend Perry Fisher.

"I don't even know if it matters, but you said to report everything. . . . I saw Kip Carter riding in Mr. Bullard's car with Mr. Bullard. . . . I don't know where they were going."

Abby made her notes.

"Number seven reporting . . ." It was Bev. "Mr. Bullard's car was gone from the school parking lot from two in the afternoon. . . . It was still gone when I went home after school."

Abby wrote it down.

"Hey, babe." It was a boy's voice. "It's number three. . . . I don't like being number three . . . you know I'm number one . . . Ha, ha! . . . Anyway it's seven o'clock at night. Bullard just went into the Trents' house."

Number three was Carly Clark. He was black and had gone to school in Cabot as a Metco student since first grade. He was a really good basketball player, good enough for a scholarship, and his parents had rented a house in Cabot, right across from the Trents, so they could keep him in school here, and let him practice, and not waste half his day coming back and forth from Boston. When they moved in, there were some people that didn't like it. But there was no real trouble.

"Hey, Abby . . . you know who this is. . . . I seen Mr. Bullard talking with Mr. Malcolm, the construction teacher, for, like, half an hour outside Bullard's office this morning."

Abby did know who it was. Tank's voice was still boyish and sort of high for a kid so big.

Abby put the information down. She used a Sharpie

with lavender ink that matched the lines on her notepaper. Alone at night in her bedroom with an earpiece plugged into her cell phone, she wrote carefully, in a nice hand, the trivial information about Bullard and other people. It was engrossing. And she felt a little edge of excitement as she wrote and watched the shape of Bullard's behavior begin to form. If you knew enough about a person, every day, if enough people watched him, you could figure out a lot of stuff.

But for now she wasn't doing any figuring. She was merely recording. Later, with Terry, maybe all that she'd written down would form a pattern that mattered. She could sort of feel it starting to. Who he saw the most, where he went the most, what he did the most. It was all going to mean something sooner or later.

The phone rang. It was late. She looked at her clock—after eleven.

"Number three again, babe. I'm going to hit the sack, but I just wanted to tell you that Bullard's still over at Trents' house."

"You're sure?"

"Sure. I can see his car. He parked it around the corner, up the street, but I can see it from my bedroom window."

"I wonder why he parked it up the street?"

"Hey, I just the spotter here, babe. You and your boyfriend s'pposed to do the thinking."

"He's not my boyfriend," Abby said.

"Uh-huh," Carly said.

"Was there space to park closer?"

"Sure," Carly said. "Park in the driveway like most people do who're visiting."

"So what do you think?"

Carly laughed.

"Well, maybe they got some hanky-panky going on," he said.

"You think he's visiting Mrs. Trent?"

"Can't tell," Carly said.

"Well, keep an eye on them," Abby said.

"Sho'," Carly said, and hung up.

Hanky-panky, she thought.

Abby sat looking at the darkness outside her bedroom window.

We'll find out, she thought.

CHAPTER 26

"Today we going to do some fists of fury," George told Terry. "We going to move round the heavy bag to the left and we going to keep hitting it as fast as we can. . . . Left-right combo, bang, bang."

George hit the bag left-right. The second punch was almost synonymous with the first.

"Like that," George said. "Bang, bang."

Terry started.

"Punch quicker," George said. "The right should land a half second after the left."

Terry punched left-right, left-right.

"Better," George said.

Terry kept punching.

"Feel it?" George said. "There's a rhythm to it."

"Bang, bang," Terry said.

"Keep your feet under you," George said. "Keep them spaced, push off the floor."

Terry moved left as he pounded the bag. He could feel the sweat begin to gather along his arms and shoulders. George was right, once he began to feel the stuttered rhythm of the punches, they came faster. It wasn't so much bang, bang as ba-bang, ba-bang.

"Okay, now move round the bag to the right, same deal. Bang, bang."

Terry was breathing hard.

"Easy for you," he gasped.

The change in direction had messed up his rhythm, and it took him a couple of circuits of the bag to get it back. Then he made one full circle of the bag in good ba-bang.

"Okay," George said. "Round one, take a seat."

Terry sat on the folding chair in the corner, his chest heaving, his arms and shoulders glistening with sweat. The sweat beaded on his face. George toweled him off and squirted a little water into Terry's mouth.

"Don't want to dehydrate," George said. "You get dehydrated and it take the zip right out of you."

Terry nodded.

"Funny, just changing directions got me screwed up on the fists of fury thing," he said.

"Why you have to do it so much," George said. "Get your muscles grooved into it."

"And nobody's even trying to hit me," Terry said.

"Time for that will come," George said. "Now we just getting grooved in."

"But . . . I mean in a real fight some guy comes at you

throwing them as fast as he can. . . . Don't you kind of feel like wait a minute, wait a minute?"

"Couple answers to that," George said. "One, that happen whether you know how to box or not, so you may as well know. Second thing is you get enough training you can maybe weather that first couple minutes until the guy runs out of steam."

Terry nodded.

"Yeah, yeah," he said. "I know. Backpedal. Keep him off with your jab. Cover up."

"And maybe move around him a little, try not to get cornered," George said. "He gonna be pretty tired after a minute or two. 'Less you fighting Smokin' Joe Frazier, your man can't keep throwing them like you talkin' about for very long."

"You ever just wanted to run?"

George shrugged.

"Boxing be mostly about training," he said. "Remember what I tol' you about the three thousand punches. Time you get in the ring, you might be scared, but you trained so much, you sort of can't think 'bout running."

"But what if you do run?"

"Then you need to do another business," George said. "Nothing wrong with that. Boxing ain't exactly normal anyway. You know, it ain't normal to get into a thing where you and somebody else try to beat each other unconscious. Don't mean you a coward or anything if you can't do it."

George paused and framed his words and smiled.

"Probably just mean you too normal for boxing."

"Aren't some fighters scared?"

"Sure," George said. "And you can be a pretty good fighter even if you scared. Technique take you a long way. But it don't take you all the way."

"What does that?" Terry said.

"Heart," George said.

"Heart?"

"Heart make you get up when it be much easier to stay down," George said. "Make you go out for the next round when you can't hardly see and you not sure where you are. We don't know yet, you got heart. But I'm thinking you might."

Neither of them spoke. George seemed to have gone someplace out of the little gym across from the Coffee Café in the fancy town. Someplace Terry had never been. Then he came back and smiled at Terry.

"Maybe just another word for not normal," he said.

CHAPTER 27

It was a warm Saturday morning and they were sitting on the rocks near the ocean, looking at what Abby called her spy chart.

"These are all the people we've seen him with in a month," Abby said. "And the places he saw them."

"That whole list?" Terry said.

"Yes," Abby said. "But they're in order of frequency. That's what the numbers in parentheses mean. See, he's seen Kip Carter All-American twelve times. He's seen Mr. Malcolm the construction teacher ten times, and so on."

"So the end of the list doesn't probably mean much."

"Probably not," Abby said. "But I put them in. Just in case."

"Damn," Terry said. "You've been putting in a lot of work."

Abby nodded.

"And these are the places we've seen him go," she said,

"where he just went there and we didn't really see him with anybody."

"Like the supermarket," Terry said.

"Exactly."

"Or the Trent house. You don't know who he sees there?"

"Carly never knows," Abby said.

"But he's been there, what, eight times?"

"That Carly has seen."

"And Carly can't tell if it's Mr. or Mrs. or both?"

"No. Carly thinks it might be hanky-panky, but he doesn't know."

"Carly thinks everything is hanky-panky," Terry said. "It's kind of hard to imagine."

"I could imagine her," Abby said. "You even said once she was kind of hot."

"With him?" Terry said. "That's what I can't imagine."

"God no," Abby said. "I can't imagine him doing it with anybody."

"And don't want to," Terry said.

"Grown-ups do have affairs, though," Abby said.

"But Bullard is married."

"Married grown-ups do have affairs, though," Abby said.

Terry nodded, looking at the way the light glanced off the moving ocean.

"I guess we need to find out," he said.

"You think it's important?"

"I think we don't know, so we need to find out."

"Yes," Abby said. "That's the right way to think."

Terry looked at the list again.

"Wow," he said. "You been doing this, like, full time."

"Pretty much," Abby said.

"How you gonna stay on the honor roll?" he said.

"Oh, phoo," she said. "You don't have to do much to make honor roll."

Terry laughed.

"You got that right," he said. "Tank made it this term."

"I rest my case," Abby said.

Terry was still studying the list.

"Okay," Terry said. "He's seen Kip Carter the most and Mr. Malcolm the next most."

"That we know about," Abby said. "We don't see him all the time."

"I know," Terry said. "I just don't want to keep saying 'as far as we know' every time."

"Just so you remember," Abby said.

"I remember," Terry said. "I remember."

"Well," Abby said. "Aren't we grouchy."

"I'm sorry. I just feel some stress, I suppose. I mean Mr. Bullard's always looking at me, and Kip Carter is always looking at me. And, you know. I mean what are we doing?"

"We're trying to find out what happened to Jason," Abby said.

Terry nodded.

"Maybe what they say happened, happened," he said.

Abby was quiet for a moment. Several seabirds lingered in the area, in search of food. Sitting close so they could both look at the charts, Terry could feel the slight pressure of Abby's thigh against his own. After a time, Abby shook her head slowly.

"No," she said. "We already know whatever happened wasn't what they say."

"Like Mr. Bullard telling me not to ask about it . . ."

"And Kip Carter All-American telling you to back off," Abby said.

"I'm not crazy," Terry said. "There's something going on, isn't there?"

"Yes," Abby said. "There is."

"And we're the only ones who know it?"

"We're the only ones that know it and are willing to do something about it," Abby said.

"And we're kids," Terry said.

"I guess," Abby said. "Sort of."

They were quiet again. The sun was warm. The ocean smelled fresh. One of the gulls hopped close and cocked its head and stared at them with its blank black eyes.

"If we're together when we're grown," Terry said, "I will never have an affair."

"Except with me," Abby said.

"That wouldn't be an affair," Terry said.

"You never know," Abby said.

CHAPTER 28

Terry stood in the dark with Abby among some evergreen shrubs in back of the Trent house.

"Carly says Bullard arrived here at seven," Abby said. "That was his car around the corner, right?"

"Yep," Terry said.

"Why would he park there if he wasn't trying to sneak?"

"Don't know," Terry said.

"Are you scared?" Abby said.

"No."

"Nervous?"

"No," Terry said. "I'm trying to think."

"Oh," Abby said. "So maybe I should shut up."

"Uh-huh," Terry said.

They stood in the dark looking at the house.

"I feel like a peeping Tom," Terry said.

"I know," Abby said. "It's kind of exciting, though."

"No lights on upstairs," Terry said.

"If they're having an affair," Abby said, "they wouldn't go right upstairs, for heaven's sake."

"What would they do?"

"Have cocktails or something, in the living room."

"You think?" Terry said.

"That's where the lights are on," Abby said.

"How do you know it's the living room?"

"'Cause I know," Abby said. "Want to peek in?"

"I guess," Terry said.

They walked carefully in the shadow of the shrubs to the back window, where the light was on, and looked in.

"Ohmigod," Abby whispered.

She stepped quickly away from the window.

"They're . . ." she said. "Are they . . . ?"

"They are," Terry whispered.

"For god's sake stop looking," Abby said.

"Why?"

"It's too embarrassing," Abby whispered. "What if they catch us?"

"I think we caught them," Terry said.

"I mean it, Terry," Abby said. "I want to go."

She pulled at his arm.

"Wow!" Terry said. "Look at that."

"No," Abby said.

She pulled harder at his arm.

"I want to go," Abby said.

"Okay," Terry said.

They walked silently away through the dark shrubs

to the street. As they walked beneath the streetlights, it seemed very bright to them.

"Mr. Bullard and Mrs. Trent," Terry said.

"I know," Abby said.

"I wonder what it means?" Terry said.

"She's the head of the town selectmen," Abby said.

"And they're connected," Terry said.

"So to speak," Abby said.

Terry grinned at her.

"Give you any ideas?" he said.

"You and I will never do anything that looks anything like that," she said.

"I think that's what it looks like," Terry said.

"Well, we don't look like that."

"I guess not," Terry said.

They continued on, in and out of the light circles spread by the streetlamps.

"Plus," Terry said. "I woulda taken my socks off."

"Ohhh," Abby said.

She punched him in the arm, not hard . . . and began to giggle.

CHAPTER 29

If that ever gets out, Mrs. Trent won't be governor," Terry said.

"I know, but what does that have to do with Jason?" Abby said.

"Maybe nothing," Terry said. "Wouldn't help Bullard's career, either, if this got around."

They were sitting on the Wall. Across the street, on the town common, two squirrels chased each other around a tree trunk.

"What should we do?" Abby said.

"I think we should focus on him and her for a while," Terry said.

"Because they're having an affair?"

"Yeah. If they're doing that, what else might they be doing?"

"He's married," Abby said. "Right?"

"Yeah. I saw her once at school, I forget what she was doing there."

"What's she like?" Abby said.

"Mrs. Bullard? She looks like someone who would marry Mr. Bullard."

"Oh dear," Abby said. "Are we going to tell anybody?"

"Oh it's too good to keep quiet," Terry said.

"No," Abby said. "We shouldn't tell."

"No?"

"Because it's too good to keep quiet. We tell Tank or Suzi or somebody and it'll be all over town."

"And that's bad?"

"It's bad if they haven't done anything else bad," Abby said. "I mean maybe they're both unhappily married, you know, and they've found each other. I mean maybe they're in love."

Terry nodded for a time.

"Yeah," he said. "We can always use it if we need to."

"You're not very romantic," Abby said.

"Am too," Terry said.

"Not about Mr. Bullard and Mrs. Trent."

"No," Terry said. "Not about them."

"Would you have stayed and watched if I hadn't been there?" Abby said.

"Sure."

"Why?"

"It was sex," Terry said. "And I'm a guy. I wanted to watch her."

"That's it?"

"Sure," Terry said. "You weren't interested?"

"I'm interested in sex, I guess," Abby said. "But not like that. I want, you know, I want some feeling in it, something romantic. I'm a girl."

"They might have had feeling in it," Terry said.

"But I didn't," Abby said.

"Not all girls are like that."

"No," Abby said. "I know. Suzi's already hooking up. Lotta girls."

"But not you," Terry said.

"I won't hook up just to hook up," Abby said.

"Because you need to be in love?"

"I guess," Abby said. "I need to feel something. It needs to matter."

"More than just the fun of it?"

"Yes," Abby said. "If it were only about fun, for me, it wouldn't be fun. Does that make any sense?"

"Not the kind of sense I wish it did," Terry said.

"I know."

"You feel something for me?" Terry said.

"Yes."

"I matter," Terry said.

Abby nodded.

"Yes," she said.

"But?"

"Not yet," Abby said.

"Not yet?"

"No."

"Why not?"

"I don't know," Abby said. "I just know that you and I are about more than just *fun*."

"Yes," Terry said. "I know that too."

"We're not very old, we have time," Abby said.

"We're old enough to know something about each other," Terry said.

"Yes."

"We are sure about each other," Terry said.

"Yes, we are."

They looked at each other and then Terry smiled.

"So, sooner or later?" he said.

Abby smiled at him and put her hand on his forearm.

"Sooner or later," Abby said.

CHAPTER 30

Okay," George said. "You're fighting two guys."

They were at the heavy bag.

"You do left jab, right cross, left hook on the bag, you pivot on me, keep your right foot planted, and throw the same punches at me and pivot back."

George grinned.

"Just in case the guy didn't go down," he said.

"Hard to believe," Terry said.

"Okay," George said. "First on the heavy bag, then on me."

Terry hit the bag, left-right, left hook, turning into each punch with his hip.

"Now me," George said.

He held the mitts up.

"Like basketball," George said. "Keep your pivot foot."

They worked on the doubling up for a while.

Then George said, "Excellent. Take a seat."

Terry slumped onto the chair. George began to help him off with the gloves.

"I need to sort something out, George," Terry said as his breathing settled.

"Uh-huh."

"You said that having heart was maybe being abnormal," Terry said.

"Uh-huh."

"Talk to me more about that," Terry said.

"Your breathing get back to normal pretty quick now, you notice that?" George said.

"Yeah, I guess I'm starting to get in shape."

George nodded.

"You are," he said.

Terry waited. He knew George had heard the question. He walked over to the shelf and put Terry's big gloves on the top shelf.

"Heart got something to do with courage, and something to do with being cruel," George said.

He turned and came back.

"You got to be willing to bash somebody in the face, maybe somebody you don't even know. You gotta do more than be willing to, you got to *want* to bash him in the face as hard and as often as you can until you win."

"That's cruel," Terry said.

"Probably is," George said. "And you got to *want* to do that while he trying to do the same thing to you."

"That's maybe the courage part?" Terry said.

George thought about it.

"It is," he said after a while. "But you also got to have the courage to be cruel."

"You don't seem cruel, George."

"Just when I fight," George said. "Got to be able to control the cruel part. It control you and you ain't a good fighter, and you ain't a good man."

"Does it bother you being cruel?"

"Not when I fighting," George said. "Ain't a matter of right and wrong anymore. You thought it was wrong, you shouldn't be doing it. You decided it was right to fight and right to win when you stepped into the ring. Now you got to do the things you got to do to get there."

"So if you're trying to do the right thing, you might need to be cruel to do it," Terry said.

George stared thoughtfully at Terry for a moment. Then he nodded.

"Yeah," he said. "If we talking 'bout fighting."

"We are," Terry said. "Sort of."

CHAPTER 31

In the early evening, while there was still light, they sat on a stone outcropping on the building site and looked at the nearly finished house. The house was closed in. The windows and doors were in. The front door had a large No Trespassing sign on it. There was still landscaping to be done, and painting, and who knew what inside. But they could see it was a nice house.

"Said in the news today that she's probably gonna win the election," Abby said.

"Trent?"

"Yes."

"Unless we blab," Terry said.

"Why would you do that?" Abby said. "Just 'cause you saw her with Bullard? That doesn't mean she shouldn't be governor."

"We don't know what it means," Terry said. "Yet."

"No," Abby said. "And until we do, we have no right to ruin anybody's life."

"I know," Terry said.

"Besides, we'd have to tell we were peeking in their window."

"We could say it was me," Terry said. "We wouldn't have to mention you."

"And they'd both deny it," Abby said. "They'd tell everybody you're a troublemaker."

"But *you're* not," Terry said.

"No, I'm a good girl. Honor roll. Never in trouble."

"So if we tell, it needs to be both of us," Terry said.

"I think so."

Terry nodded.

"We'll keep our mouths shut for the moment, I guess."

"They're both pretty interested in this project," Abby said. "They each come here three, four times a week. Sometimes they're both here. Sometimes one, sometimes the other."

"I thought this was conservation land," Terry said.

"So?"

"So I think that means you aren't supposed to build on it."

"Probably okay if it's a school project," Abby said.

"So what happens to the house when it's built?" Terry said.

"I don't know."

"Me neither."

"It would be nice to know," Abby said.

"Depends on who you ask, I guess," Terry said. "I got in trouble asking about steroids."

"I know," Abby said.

"It's frustrating as hell," Terry said. "We're pretty sure that Jason didn't commit suicide. We're pretty sure that there's something going on with Bullard, and Trent and Kip Carter. There's something going on with this house."

"We're sure something's going on between Trent and Bullard," Abby said.

"And that's all we know," Terry said. "We can't prove anything except that, and who knows if anyone will believe us."

"Plus we have to fess up that we were spying on them," Abby said. "And then we might have to explain why and tell about our spy network and . . . Terry, a lot of people could get in trouble."

Terry nodded.

It was beginning to get dark. They stood and walked back out the dirt road from the construction site. As they went, Terry noticed some Day-Glo orange painted stakes in the ground along the road.

"Look at the stakes," he said to Abby.

"What are they for?" Abby said.

"It looks like they're marking out where to build other houses."

"On conservation land?"

"I guess," Terry said.

CHAPTER 32

Abby asked Nancy Fortin the next day, and Nancy Fortin asked around among the other kids in the technical arts curriculum. But nobody knew what happened to the project houses after they were built.

"If I was you," Nancy said, "I'd go down to the tech arts office and talk to Mr. Malcolm. He's the house master."

So Abby went to the technical arts office and asked for Mr. Malcolm.

He was in.

"So," he said. "Miss Hall, what is your interest in technical arts?"

"It's really just curiosity, Mr. Malcolm. I was walking in the woods last night with my dog, and I saw that house that your department is building, and I thought, *Wow!* I got to find out about this."

"Why are you interested?"

"Well," Abby said, "it's so fabulous. I mean that kids are building something like that."

Mr. Malcolm smiled and nodded. He was lean and had short gray hair and a sort of healthy outdoor look.

"Yes," he said. "We're very proud of the program. It's one of the few full-scale construction programs in the state."

"I'm sorry I sound so stupid," Abby said. "But have you built many?"

"No," Malcolm said. "It's a new program. Mr. Bullard brought me in to run it."

"And you know about construction?"

"Yes," he said, and smiled at her. "I have been a contractor for more than thirty years. I'm able to hire a lot of my subcontractors on a per diem basis to serve as instructors in various phases."

"You mean like plumbers for the plumbing part and electrical guys for the electricity part?"

Malcolm nodded happily.

"Exactly," he said. "Normally skilled tradesmen aren't available to teach, because, quite frankly, they make too much doing what they do to give it up for teaching. But if I can hire them between jobs and pay them well, but not for very long, we can get expert faculty in all phases of the construction without huge costs."

"Wow, again!" Abby said. "Is that your idea?"

"Well, I have a part in it. Because of my long experience, I know a great many subs . . . subcontractors," he said. "But the plan originated, I believe, with Mr. Bullard. Mrs. Trent, when she was chair of the school committee, and more recently, as chairperson of the selectmen, has been very supportive."

"Is somebody who's gone through this program ready to work when he graduates?" Abby said.

She was leaning forward, her eyes wide, giving every evidence of being totally fascinated.

"Absolutely," Mr. Malcolm said. "They've had hands-on training from experts. Incidentally it's not just *he* anymore. It could be *she*, you know."

"And do you help them get jobs?" Abby said.

"In cooperation with the guidance office," Mr. Malcolm said. "Plus, I have so many contacts in the building business that I can be quite helpful in a more informal way."

Abby appeared entranced.

"Fabulous," she said. "What a fabulous program."

Mr. Malcolm smiled at her enthusiasm.

"It's been a dream project of mine for many years," he said. "And now that I don't have to devote so much time to my own business, I have the chance to see the dream come true."

"That's really great," Abby said. "What do you do with the house when it's finished?"

"Finished?" Malcolm said.

"Yes, it's so great . . . really fabulous. . . . Do you do something special?"

"We . . . ah . . . You'll have talk to Mr. Bullard about that."

"Mr. Bullard?"

"Yes," Mr. Malcolm said. "He would be the one to ask."

Abby frowned in a cute way and looked puzzled.

"Don't you know?" Abby said.

"Mr. Bullard would be the one to ask about that," Mr. Malcolm said, and looked at his watch.

Abby considered that option.

I don't think so.

CHAPTER 33

You going into a fight," George said. "You know what you trying to do. You got a plan. You need to stay with the plan. Worst thing you can do is get one on the nose and get mad and go crazy and can the plan."

Terry had the big gloves off and was finishing up on the speed bag, which, as George said, was mostly for show. It was somewhat useful for hand-eye coordination, Terry knew, and it was kind of an aerobic workout.

"What if the plan isn't working?" he asked.

"Then you come up with another one. What you don't do is just get mad and start whaling away," George said. "That ain't no plan and it will get you hurt."

"Didn't you ever get mad?"

"You get mad, you use it for energy," George said. "You control it and channel it. Otherwise you lose your technique, and you don't stay over your feet, and you let yourself get off balance and overextended and you get your clock cleaned and your ticket punched pretty quick."

"What if the other guy is mad too?" Terry said.

"Then the control is gone," George said. "Then it just a brawl and a lucky punch win it."

Terry finished up on the speed bag.

"Now deck him," George said.

Terry got the bag moving again and then hit it as hard as he could with a right overhand punch.

"A devastating punch," George said. "Now take a seat and breathe."

Terry sat on the folding chair and began to peel the self-stick trainer's tape off his hands.

"It's all about control, isn't it, George?" Terry said.

"It is," George said.

He pushed the wastebasket closer so Terry could drop the used tape in it and took the big sixteen-ounce boxing gloves to the shelf.

"Hard for a kid," Terry said, "to control stuff."

"It is," George said. "Most of the time people controlling you."

"Was that the way it was for you?"

"When I was a kid," George said, "there was no control. Kid needs some. I didn't get none 'til the priest started me boxing."

"Then you could control things, 'cause you could fight," Terry said.

"I could control myself," George said. "So can you. It's the only control matters."

"Self-control."

"Sure," George said. "You maybe want to fight Golden Gloves, fine. You maybe want to go on and fight pro, fine. I'll stay with you far as you want. But I ain't teaching you to box so you'll be a good boxer."

"Then what the hell are you teaching me for?" Terry said.

"So you be a good man."

"Not a good man because I can box," Terry said.

"That's correct," George said.

"A good man because I can control myself," Terry said.

"That's correct," George said.

"'Cause I can stick with my plan."

"First you learn to have a plan. Then you learn to stick to it until it proves to be wrong. Then you get a new plan."

"You're talking about life," Terry said.

"You need to have the smarts to know your best interest," George said. "And you need to have the control to stay with it."

"So," Terry said slowly, "everything won't be a brawl that's decided by a lucky punch."

George smiled and hit the speed bag, his hands so fast that Terry could barely see them. The movement of the bag was pyrotechnic and entirely rhythmic.

"Badda bing," George said.

CHAPTER 34

On her way home from school Friday, Abby passed the dirt road that led to the construction project. She stopped for a moment and listened. She didn't hear anything. It was after school hours, so there was probably nobody working on the project. Sometimes when you looked at a thing, Abby thought, and tried to keep your mind empty, you would think of something. She turned into the quiet dirt road and walked to the site. It was empty. She stood looking at it, listening to the bird sounds in the empty woods. The house was a big one, and fancy.

Worth a lot of money . . . to someone . . . Maybe it got sold and the money went back into the school budget . . . or the town budget . . . if the town had a budget . . . it must, towns cost money . . . so how come nobody seems to know who got the money? Except maybe Mr. Bullard and she didn't dare ask him.

She heard a footstep behind her and turned and it was

Kip Carter. She felt the little jag of fear flash through the center of her stomach.

"Little Abby Hall," he said. "Out in the woods all alone."

Abby stared at him. He was like a grown man, big, with muscles. He looked like he shaved every day. And he was handsome in a pouty self-satisfied kind of way that Abby hated. She also hated that she was afraid of him.

"What do you want?" she said.

"I was going to ask you the same thing," Kip Carter said.

"I don't want anything," Abby said.

"Maybe I do," Kip Carter said.

"I don't care if you do or not," Abby said.

He moved closer to her. She felt the fear. But she felt anger too. She started to walk around him. He stepped in front of her.

"Where you going?" he said.

"I'm going home," Abby said, and started to move past him again.

Kip Carter stepped in front of her again.

"We need a little talk," he said.

Abby moved to go around him in the other direction. He stayed in her way. It was almost like a dance step.

"About what?" Abby said.

"About why you're snooping around this construction site. About why you're asking nosy questions about what happens when it's done. About what you and your creepy boyfriend are up to in general."

"Terry's not my boyfriend and he's not creepy."

"Yeah? I say he is."

"Gordon didn't think so," Abby said.

"Gordon." Kip Carter laughed. "Your creep boyfriend gets in a lucky punch and now people think he's tough. He's a kid. He annoys me and I'll step on him like he's a cockroach."

"I don't want to talk to you," Abby said.

She moved again. He stepped in her way again.

"What are you two little nerds up to?" he said.

"We're not nerds," Abby said. "And we're not up to anything. Now get out of my way."

Kip Carter laughed.

"Who you telling to get out of your way?" he said.

They danced the little dance again. Kip Carter seemed to be liking it. Abby felt equal parts fear and anger and both were growing.

"You ain't going no place," Kip Carter said. "Until you tell me why you're asking about this property."

She tried to dodge around him again and he put a hand against her chest and shoved her. She staggered back and a branch scratched across her face. The pain made her madder. She tried to run past him. He pushed her again and she fell down.

He said, "Bad things can happen to little girls in the woods, you know."

She scrambled to her feet. Her face felt hot. He put a hand on each side of her face and put his face close. He shook her head slightly.

"Now," he said, "what's going on?"

She hit him in the mouth with her right fist. It cut his lip and the blood spurted. He swore and let go of her face and she dodged around him and ran for the street. He stood for a moment, stunned that she had hit him, looking at the blood on his hands as if he couldn't believe it.

"You cut my lip," he said.

Then he started after her. He was faster than she was. But the stunned moment cost him and she reached the street before he could catch her.

He screamed at her.

"This isn't over. I'll get you. I'm gonna get you."

There were people on the street. A woman, seeing the boy emerge bleeding from the woods, stopped and spoke to him.

"Are you all right?" she said. "Do you need help?"

Kip Carter shook his head, looking after Abby.

Abby kept going.

CHAPTER 35

After school on Monday she walked down to the Wall to
meet Terry. She had covered the long scratch on her cheek
as best she could, with makeup. She wouldn't tell him, she
decided. It would upset him. It might even cause trouble.
Kip Carter was three years older than Terry and much bigger. What if Terry felt obliged to fight with him? Plus she
didn't want to talk about it. She didn't even like to think
about it. Thinking about it made her want to cry.

Terry was on the Wall when she got there. She sat beside him.

"Hi," he said.

"Hi."

"What happened to your face?" he said.

"Nothing," she said.

"You got a scratch right across your whole cheek,"
he said.

"It's just a scratch," she said.

"I can see that," Terry said. "How'd you get it?"

She felt it coming. She tried to stop it. She couldn't. She turned her head away and started to cry.

"What?" Terry said.

She cried harder. He felt something like panic.

"Why are you crying?" Terry said.

She shook her head.

He slid off the Wall and walked around so he could look at her.

"Why are you crying?" he said.

She put her hands over her face.

"Don't look at me," she said.

"Why?"

He didn't know what to do. He put his hand on her shoulder. She felt how red her eyes must be, and puffy. Her nose had started to run. She wiped it with her sleeve.

"Don't look," she said again.

He went back and sat where he'd been and she cried with her back to him. After a time she fished a packet of tissues from her backpack and tried to clean up her face. Then she got out some makeup and a little mirror and did some damage control. Finally she got her breathing back under control and turned to Terry.

"I'm sorry," she said.

"What happened?" Terry said.

She shook her head.

"Oh for god's sake, Abby," Terry said. "You can't do

that. You can't have a major meltdown in front of me and not tell me why."

She clasped her hands and looked down at her thumbs for a time. Then she looked up at Terry and nodded.

"No," she said. "I can't."

He waited. She took in some breath and let it out slowly.

Then she told him.

He listened in absolute silence. His body motionless. His gaze fixed on her face. He felt himself slowly getting colder inside, as if he were turning to ice. He thought, *I'm going to have to do something about this*. He felt threading through the cold a small wiggle of uncertainty. He wasn't sure what he should do about it . . . or could.

When Abby got through, they sat in silence, until Abby said, "What do you think of that?"

Terry thought about his answer.

"I . . . I can't let it go."

"Why?"

"I can't," Terry said. "I can't just let him treat you like that."

"I don't . . . I would hate it if you got into trouble with him. I would feel awful, because I told you."

"But I can't let him do that," Terry said again.

"It's about me," Abby said. "Not you."

"It's about us," Terry said.

Abby started to speak and stopped. They were quiet again.

"Everything is about us," Terry said.

Abby nodded.

I'm fifteen, she thought, *how the hell am I supposed to know what to say?*

"What are you going to do?" Abby said.

"I don't know," Terry said. "But I gotta do something."

"We're doing something," Abby said. "We'll keep doing it."

"I can't let him bother you again," Terry said.

"What do you think George would say?"

"George?" Terry said.

"Yeah, George," she said. "What would George tell you to do?"

"He'd say I needed to make sure you were safe."

"How would he say to do that?"

Terry thought about George.

You need to stay with the plan. Worst thing you can do is . . . get mad and go crazy. . . . You get mad, you use it for energy. . . . You control it and channel it. . . . You need to have the control.

Terry nodded slowly.

"I know what to do," Terry said.

CHAPTER 36

They went across the common to the town library and sat at the farthest table back and worked softly on their plan. They stayed until suppertime.

That night both of them made many phone calls.

The next day Abby typed up the whole plan on her computer and ran off a bunch of pages and stapled them together. She liked organizing, being neat, getting everything in order.

That afternoon, when school was over, they gathered, eleven of them including Terry and Abby, at the rocks by the town beach, away from everybody, where no one could hear them or approach them without being seen. It was the inner circle of the spy ring. Otis was there, looking worried, and Tank, and Nancy, who seemed ill at ease with the other kids. Perry Fisher was there and Bev, and Suzi, the wind ruffling her big hair. Steve Bellino stood with

Mitchell and Carly Clark, who was taller than the rest of them, and darker.

"Okay," Terry said. "Like I said on the phone, we're gonna make our move on this whole thing we been spying. We're gonna do it today, and Abby and I will do all the hard stuff. Abby will give you your letter packets. Hang on to them. And we need you to stick around with us in case somebody gets nasty. It's pretty hard to be too bad in front of eleven eyewitnesses."

"Might be able to do better than be a witness," Carly Clark said.

"You got that right," Tank said.

"We're not looking for trouble," Abby said. "If we're together, nobody much is going to give us any."

"We don't want people thinking we're a bunch of hooligans," Otis said.

Everybody looked at him.

"Hooligans?" Steve Bellino said. "What kinda word is that?"

Otis shrugged and looked at the ocean.

"Hey," Carly said. "We all in this together. Otis wanna say 'hooligan' he can say 'hooligan,' you know?"

"You're right," Bellino said. "Hey, Otis, I'm sorry. I was only kidding you."

"It's okay," Otis said, and smiled.

"We need to stay together as much as we can," Abby said. "I got a sort of plan in with the letters packet about where to meet so we can walk to school together, and where Terry and I are going to go, and where to meet us, stuff like that."

"I know," Terry said, "that all eleven of us can't be together all the time. But several of us can."

"And we all got cell phones," Suzi said. "One phone call and we all come running."

"You're each, like, sort of team captains," Abby said. "And you each got your list of people you call, you know, like in a snowstorm."

"You bet," Suzi said.

Suzi looked like she was planning for her wedding. Her eyes were bright. She was excited. Suzi was adventurous, Terry knew. For Suzi this was fun.

Terry felt a tightness in his throat as he stood in front of them, with the quiet ocean moving behind him, and the mild breeze blowing past. He felt like he loved all these people, some of whom he barely knew, and in other circumstances might have been scornful of. He knew he wasn't a very scornful guy, but these people covered a pretty good spectrum. Perry was probably queer. Otis was a nerd. Carly was a basketball star. Tank was very big. Suzi was a sexpot. Bev was some sort of goody-goody. Bellino was mainstream. Mitchell was . . . hell, he didn't know anything about Mitchell.

"So if we really have to," Abby continued, "I figure we can pull about forty people together."

"Easy," Tank said. "Everybody likes Abby, and nobody likes Kip Carter. It's a no-brainer."

"Anyway," Terry said. "I just want to thank you for standing up for us."

"And Jason," Perry said.

Terry nodded.

"And Jason," he said.

"Hell, Terry," Tank said. "This is fun."

"Yeah," Carly said, "and who you rather have fun with than Carter and Bullard."

"And maybe Old Lady Trent," Bev said.

Everyone turned and looked at her.

"Bev?" Suzi said.

"Well, I don't like her," Bev said.

He knew they were right. For most of them this was like a war game, like cops and robbers, but maybe it wasn't for Perry. And for him and for Abby it had kept getting more serious. But for the rest . . . cowboys and Indians . . . Didn't matter. It was a good feeling to have them there.

Terry smiled.

"Okay," he said. "Let's saddle up."

CHAPTER 37

Everyone knew it was an election ploy. But Mrs. Trent kept open-door office hours at her campaign headquarters on Main Street, from three to six every day. The office was in a storefront a block up the street from the Coffee Café. At 4:10, Terry and Abby arrived with seven other kids. The seven others waited outside. Across the street, standing inside the entrance to the movie theater, Kip Carter watched Terry and Abby go into the storefront. There was no one in the office but Mrs. Trent and some staff. A Cabot police cruiser was parked outside. The outer office was plastered with campaign posters that said:

SALLY TRENT FOR GOVERNOR

and showed a big picture of the candidate in a white blouse and some pearls.

"Do you kids want to see our next governor?" a young woman said to them. She was seated at a table behind a bank of telephones.

"Yes ma'am," Abby said.

"Are you supporters?" the young woman said.

"Of course," Terry said.

"That's great," the young woman said. She turned to a young guy in jeans and a plaid shirt who sat with his feet up at the next table and said, "Get some pictures of this, Harry."

She stood and went to the inner office door and spoke. In a moment she nodded and turned back.

"Come on in, kids," she said. "Mrs. Trent would love to see you."

As they walked to Mrs. Trent's office, Harry the camera guy stood and came in behind them.

Abby murmured to Terry, "Let them take their pictures first."

Terry nodded. They went in.

Sally Trent's office was smaller than the outer one. Just a desk, two guest chairs, and a phone. On the walls were more campaign posters, including some that said:

LET'S RALLY BEHIND SALLY

As they came in, she stood and walked around her desk. She was wearing a tailored gray suit and a French blue shirt with a long collar. The collar was open over the pearls at her throat. Abby already could see that the pearls, which Terry probably hadn't noticed, were Mrs. Trent's trademark. She glanced at Harry, then smiled at Terry and Abby.

"Young supporters, how lovely," she said.

She glanced at the camera, saw that it was ready, and put out her hand.

"Tell me your names," she said.

"Terry Novak."

"Abby Hall."

Mrs. Trent shook both their hands. The camera clicked and flashed as she was doing it.

"Terry and Abby," she said with an even bigger smile. "If only you could vote."

"We will in a while," Abby said.

"Yes," Mrs. Trent said. "You are the future."

They stood uneasily for a moment. Mrs. Trent glanced at the young woman assistant, who nodded slightly toward the two chairs. She made a talking gesture with her thumb and fingers.

"Do sit down," Mrs. Trent said. "Give me how things look from your perspective."

The woman stood beside the door. The cameraman stood on the other side.

"Excuse me, ma'am," Abby said. "But we have to speak with you in private."

"Uh-oh," Mrs. Trent said, and smiled harder. She looked at the assistant. The assistant nodded.

"Come on, Harry," the assistant said. "Give them a little privacy."

The assistant and the camera guy left the room. Mrs. Trent sat back down behind her desk, crossed her legs, smoothed her skirt over her knees, folded her hands in her lap, and leaned back slightly in her chair. She smiled at them brightly.

"Okay, what secrets do you have to tell me?" she said.

Here it was. The moment. Terry could feel, in the center of himself, the jagged thump of its arrival. They had rehearsed it twenty times. They had agreed that Abby would start off. It would be easier to hear, they thought, coming from Abby. And Abby was more socially graceful than Terry. She could talk better.

"We need you to help us," Abby said.

Mrs. Trent was warm.

"I will if I can," she said.

"We think something bad is going on in town, something to do with Jason Green and the construction near the Eel Pond Woods, and maybe something to do with steroids, and with Kip Carter, and Mr. Bullard."

Mrs. Trent's face began to stiffen.

"And," Abby said, "we know you're having an affair with Mr. Bullard."

Mrs. Trent's face went gray-white. She stared at them. The stiff and pointless smile began to fade away. Terry felt as if he might not be able to breathe. He looked at Abby. She seemed calm and friendly and perfectly able to breathe. Mrs. Trent's face was now the color of sea ice, the way it got sometimes when it was really cold and the harbor froze along the edges. Her mouth was open as if she were going to speak. But she didn't speak.

"Could you help us with this?" Abby said.

She stared at them some more, and as she stared, the color in her face began to reverse itself. The blood came slowly back until her face was actually flushed, and she looked almost like she might have a fever.

"How . . ." She stopped and took a breath. "How dare you come in here and say such a thing."

"We need your help," Terry said.

They had rehearsed this, too. The first time she responded to Abby, Terry would answer. After that they'd have to play it by ear.

Mrs. Trent was outraged.

"Everything you have said, everything, is a huge and disgusting lie. I cannot imagine how you think you can get away with taking my time to come in here and behave like this."

"We saw you and Mr. Bullard making love," Abby said.

Again the stare, the color shifting in her face. The sense that she might be fighting for oxygen.

"That's not possible," she said. "And the accusation is disgusting."

"You have a small blue butterfly tattooed on your butt," Terry said.

Again the long awful silence. Mrs. Trent looked at her office door. No help there. She looked at the campaign poster that said, LET'S RALLY BEHIND SALLY. Then she seemed to brace herself.

"Is this what you do?" she said finally. "You sneak around in the night like little rats and peek in windows?"

They waited.

"That kind of behavior is disgusting," she said.

Neither of them said anything.

"It's also illegal," she said. "Do you realize there's a police cruiser right outside? If I call them in, they'll arrest you right here."

They waited.

"Who would believe you?" she said.

Terry shrugged. Abby looked blank.

"It would simply be the word of two idiotic children against mine," she said.

Abby took her cell phone from her school bag and held it up.

"Why are you showing me that?" Mrs. Trent said.

"Takes pictures," Terry said.

Abby kept holding it up. Mrs. Trent kept looking at it.

After what seemed a long time, she said in a hushed voice, "You took pictures?"

"Why not," Terry said.

Again she seemed silent forever.

Then she said, "What do you want?"

CHAPTER 38

She was so close to being governor.

She was ahead in every poll. . . . Her opponent had been shooting himself in the foot since the campaign began. . . . She was a lock . . . except for these stupid little kids. . . . How could they spoil it for her. . . . She was smarter than they were, older, wiser. . . . Toughen up, Sally. . . . Think! . . . Think!

"We need you to help us," Abby said, with a nice smile. "We need you to help us figure out what happened to Jason, and what's going on at the tech arts construction site, and what's up with Mr. Bullard. . . ."

"Besides you," Terry said.

Abby smiled at his remark and kept talking.

". . . and Kip Carter, and steroids, and, things like that."

Go along with them. . . . Pretend to be with them. . . . Buy some time. . . . These are kids. . . . Don't give it up. . . . Don't quit. . . . Come on, Sally, handle it. . . . Play hardball.

She smiled.

"That seems a pretty big order," she said. "And I don't see how I can be much help. But if I could help, and did, what happens?"

"All we know disappears forever," Abby said.

Mrs. Trent nodded.

"And if I can't help you?"

"We have a letter," Terry said. "Telling everything we know and suspect. It goes to a whole bunch of newspapers and TV stations."

Terry glanced at Abby. She looked at her notebook in her lap and read aloud from her list.

"*The Globe*," she said. "*The Herald. The New Bedford Standard Times, Salem News, Lynn Item, Lowell Sun, Lawrence Eagle-Tribune, Worcester Gazette, Springfield Republican,* Channels 4, 5, 7. You get the idea."

"And," Mrs. Trent said kindly, "where are these letters now?"

"A bunch of our friends have them," Abby said. "Sealed, stamped, and addressed."

"Do they know the contents?" Mrs. Trent said, as if it didn't really matter and she was just curious.

"No," Terry said. "But they know to send the letters if anything happens to us."

Mrs. Trent widened her eyes.

"Happens to you?" she said. "My dear boy, aren't you getting a little overheated?"

She shifted in her chair.

"Something happened to Jason," Abby said.

Nice legs, though, Terry thought, *for her age.*

"I understood that was suicide," Mrs. Trent said.

Keep talking to them. . . . Work them, Sally, work them. . . . You've come too far, Sally, to let yourself be ruined by a couple of high school kids. . . . You've got them talking to you. . . . Pretty soon you can have them explaining. . . . You know how to do this, Sally, play them.

Terry looked at his watch.

"We're going to give this one more minute," he said. "Then we will get up and go out and tell our friends to mail their letters."

She stared contemptuously at Terry. Sally Trent, the most powerful woman in the state, being confronted by two stupid little kids. She wanted to spit on them.

After nearly a minute she said, "There are things I can give you."

CHAPTER 39

The female assistant stuck her head in the office door.

"Everything going well?" she asked brightly.

Mrs. Trent waved her away. The door closed again.

"Yes," Mrs. Trent said, "I have a relationship with Paxton Bullard."

Terry and Abby looked at each other.

Paxton!

"How old are you," Mrs. Trent asked, "seventeen or so?"

"We're both fifteen," Abby said.

"Well, you look older," Mrs. Trent said. "But even more to the point, you are probably not able to understand this sort of thing. But . . ." She took a breath. "Paxton is a long-time friend of my husband's. He and Gerry were friends in college. When Gerry was head of the planning board, here in Cabot, Paxton came to him with a scheme. The school had just instituted an ambitious technical arts program, one of the first of its kind in an, ah, affluent school like Dawes Regional. He had a plan to use the resources of the technical arts program to build houses for nothing, and sell them for a great deal, and keep the money. Obviously he needed the kind of help only town officials could provide."

Abby was sitting straight in her chair, with her knees and ankles together, fully absorbed in what Mrs. Trent was saying. Terry looked at her profile. He didn't know if she looked older than fifteen. But he knew she was beautiful.

"My husband is a weak man. But he is loyal to his friends and, sad to say, I guess, is a bit greedy. I was head of the selectmen at the time. He asked me to do some things that seemed innocent, and I did them for him. He did some things. And among the things he did was to imply that he was speaking for me and to sign my name to a number of documents, which, in short, allowed this project to proceed."

Neither Terry nor Abby said anything. The story was starting to be told and they didn't want to break the spell. Mrs. Trent seemed almost dreamy as she talked.

"I'm very orderly," she said. "And very careful. I was reviewing my recent activities on the board when it struck me that some of the decisions I seemed to have signed on to were specious."

Terry wasn't exactly sure what *specious* meant. But Abby would know, and until he could ask her, he had a pretty good idea from the context.

"I confronted Gerry, my husband, and he confessed to me. He begged me to let it go. He's terrified of Paxton. Most people are, I suppose. He's so big, and he has all those muscles, and he has such an explosive temper. But I have a conscience, and I have a duty to those people who elected me to represent them. So I went to Paxton, and I said, *'This has to stop, now!'*"

She paused for a moment, looking not at them really, more past them, at something that seemed far away. Terry and Abby sat motionless, waiting for her to go on.

"He laughed at me," Mrs. Trent said. "He is a troglodyte. Some sort of antediluvian beast, I think."

A couple of other words he'd have to ask Abby about.

"He said there was no paper with his name on it," Mrs. Trent went on. "He said that if we did anything to expose the scheme, he'd take my husband and myself down with him and that we'd fall a lot farther and land a lot harder."

Again she paused, again the faraway look of soft sadness.

"My husband is a weak fool, and he's not terribly bright," she said finally. "But he's my husband and I love him. I could not expose him to that, and Bullard knew it."

She had shifted from "Paxton" to "Bullard," Terry noticed.

"And then . . ." She paused again, as if she were fighting off tears. "And then he said that to cement our new conspiracy, our new partnership, so to speak . . ."

She stopped and put her hands on either side of her face and pressed, as if she were trying to keep herself together.

"He said that I had to become his mistress. . . ."

She slid her hands together and buried her face in them and sat for a long time.

"Does Mr. Malcolm know about this house thing?" Terry said.

Her voice was muffled as she spoke with her face still in her hands.

"I assume so," she said.

"How about Kip Carter?" Abby said. "Where does he fit in?"

Mrs. Trent straightened and took a Kleenex from her purse and dabbed at her eyes, carefully, so as not to disturb her makeup. Her eyes looked dry, Terry thought. Then she folded her hands, still clutching the Kleenex, and placed them in her lap.

"Paxton uses him as a kind of enforcer with the kids," she said calmly. "He helped Kip with his scholarship to Illinois. And he, I believe, supplies Kip and some of his pals with steroids. Paxton uses them himself, I know. Perhaps it accounts for his vicious temper."

"What do you mean, *enforcer*?" Abby said.

"Make sure all the kids that knew about the project didn't get nosy or talk about it the wrong way," Mrs. Trent said. "You know. If they thought something was wrong and it was the principal's fault, they might tell somebody.

But, and you probably know these rules better than I do, they wouldn't squeal on one of the other kids."

"Plus Kip Carter is the biggest wheel in the school," Abby said.

"And the toughest guy," Terry said.

"So," Abby said, "yes. You're right. Kids would much rather not rat out Kip Carter. Loyalty, fear . . ." Abby moved her hands in sort of random circles as she searched for the right word.

"Tribal loyalty, perhaps," Mrs. Trent said.

"Yes, that's right," Abby said.

"How's he get away with all this?" Terry said.

"He is both school superintendent and principal of the high school," Mrs. Trent said. "That's quite unusual. Not unheard of, but unusual. It gives him unusual autonomy."

Another one for Abby, Terry thought. *Must mean something like* power.

"And Jason?" Terry asked. "Do you know what happened to Jason Green?"

Mrs. Trent shifted again in her chair, so that she was facing more toward Terry. She crossed her legs the other way and smoothed her skirt. Then she looked up and gazed hard and straight at Terry.

"No," Mrs. Trent said. "As God is my witness. I do not know what happened to Jason Green."

CHAPTER 40

The posse of kids gathered around them as they came out of the storefront.

"What'd she say? . . . She tell you anything? . . . What'd she tell you? . . . What happened? Do we mail the letters?"

"Hang on to the letters," Terry said. "Don't mail them. Don't lose them. Just stand by on the letters."

"What'd she say?"

Terry shook his head.

"Abby and me are going to go to the café and go over what she said. Give us some time to do that, okay?"

"To the café," Tank shouted, and pointed grandly down the street. From the patrol car, the cop looked at them with mild amusement and shook his head slightly. As they trooped down the street, Sally Trent and her assistant came out of the storefront and got in a car. The car took them away, and the police car went with them. In the shadow of the theater entrance, Kip Carter stared after them.

It was a slow time in the café. Too late for lunch, too early for supper, but kind of late for a coffee and a snack. Terry and Abby went to a booth in the back and sat across from each other and ordered coffee.

"Paxton?" Terry said.

"He always signs everything P. F. Bullard," Abby said. "I never knew his name was Paxton."

"What do you suppose the 'F' stands for?" Terry asked.

"Fauntleroy?" Abby said.

They laughed and sipped their coffee.

"Do you believe what she told us?" Terry said.

"Of course not," Abby said.

"No?"

"Remember she said there were things she could give us."

"Yeah?"

"She gave us her husband and her boyfriend," Abby said.

"What don't you believe?"

"Most of it," Abby said. "For instance, say the basic events are true, and Bullard's making money off the school, and maybe distributing 'roids to some of his jock faves. . . . You think he's going to risk getting fired, maybe going to jail, and losing, what, a million dollars? On the house-building thing? You think he's going to risk all that to have sex with Sally Trent?"

"Is that what he did?"

"Sure," Abby said. "Essentially she said, he said, have sex with me or I'll turn us all in."

"She said he said that his name wasn't on any documents."

"Maybe," Abby said. "Maybe it wasn't. But if he tells his story, you think he won't get connected to it? You think he would think that?"

"No."

"Correct. So if we believe her story, he's willing to risk everything to have sex with her."

"She does have pretty good legs," Terry said.

Abby slapped his forearm.

"Stop that," she said.

He grinned at her.

"Well," he said. "One thing, when we were peeking in, while you were hiding your eyes and saying 'eek,' I was taking a look, and I don't know all that much about it, but she didn't act like she was doing anything she didn't want to do . . . you know?"

"Yuck," Abby said.

"But you do know what I mean?"

Abby blushed slightly.

"Yes," she said. "So you don't believe her either?"

Terry held his coffee mug in both hands and sipped from it while he looked at her over the rim of the mug.

"Here's what I think," he said. "I think Bullard is involved in making money out of the house-building project. I believe he takes steroids, and I bet he gives some to

Kip Carter. Mr. Trent's probably involved too. And maybe something happened to Jason because he found out about this. He was in the tech arts program, you know."

"But if Jason found out anything, would he tell Mr. Bullard?"

"He might have told Mr. Malcolm, or asked him about it, or something," Terry said. "And Malcolm told Bullard."

"Are you saying that Mr. Bullard killed Jason?" Abby said.

"I don't know. We got this bunch of illegal stuff going on and right in the middle of it Jason dies, and when we start asking about it, Bullard and Kip Carter are on us like a heavy storm."

"Why not Mr. Malcolm?"

"Possible, I suppose. But he hasn't been bothering us like Bullard . . . and not for nothing, but if someone got killed and the two suspects were Mr. Malcolm and Mr. Bullard, who would you guess?"

"Yes," Abby said. "You're right. Mr. Bullard."

"Sure," Terry said.

"So how much do you think Mrs. Trent was involved?" Abby said.

"She's in it up to her, ah, blue butterfly," Terry said.

They both laughed.

"And the rest of it, how she loves her husband, and she didn't know they were forging her name, and Bullard forced her to . . ." Abby made a face and shivered.

"Crappola," Terry said. "That's the best she could come up with at the moment. By the time it reaches the press, if it ever does, imagine how bad everyone will feel for her."

"I wonder what she'd say if she found out I didn't take a picture with my cell phone?" Abby said.

"We never said you did," Terry said.

"Not exactly."

"So I think she's in it all the way, that she probably had the affair with Bullard first, and they thought up this scheme, and she dragged her husband into it, and . . ." Terry finished his sentence by turning both palms up.

"Yeah, she's a terrible woman," Abby said. "I agree with you."

"So where do we go from here?"

"We got enough to probably ruin her chance to be governor and get Mr. Bullard fired," Abby said.

Terry nodded.

"But we started this to find out what happened to Jason," he said.

"And we still don't know," Abby said.

"No."

"And Kip Carter?" Abby asked.

"He's unfinished business," Terry said.

"Because?"

"He threatened you," Terry said.

"It doesn't bother me," Abby said. "Why should it bother you?"

"It bothers me," Terry said.

"So what do we do next?" Abby said.

"I don't know," Terry said. "But it's not over yet. We still have to find out what happened to Jason."

"And then it's over?" Abby said.

"Almost," Terry said.

Abby looked at him silently. He patted her arm.

"Maybe somebody else will do something else," Abby said.

"We stirred things up enough," Terry said. "Something ought to happen."

Kip Carter was the best running back that had ever played in this town. Himself, Kip Carter. He knew that. He was probably the best running back in the state. And he had size. At eighteen he was 6' 1" and weighed 205. He knew he could play in the Big Ten. He might even get pro size as he matured, with maybe a little help from the juice. Kip Carter was going to be somebody. Hell, he was somebody now! Every guy in school was afraid of him. Even the older townie guys didn't give him any trouble. . . . Terry Novak had to be scared of Kip Carter. So why did he keep doing stuff that Kip Carter had told him not to do? And the little alley cat girlfriend—she had actually hit him, Kip Carter, and cut his lip.

He watched the gang of kids, Novak's groupies, head down the street with Novak toward the café. He watched as Mrs. Trent came out of the office where Novak and his girlfriend had just been. Mr. Bullard wouldn't like them talking to Mrs. Trent. It was not always exactly clear to him what Mr. Bullard was doing, but he knew it had something to do with Mrs. Trent, and he knew that Bullard didn't want Novak and the girl nosing around in it. He was a little scared of Mr. Bullard. His authority. His size. His rage. But Bullard was his ticket to ride. He'd got him the scholarship to Illinois. He was the source for the 'roids, which had moved him to another level, like Bullard had said it would. And if Kip Carter had a hero, it would be Mr. Bullard.

Mr. Bullard would want to know about this. He'd want to nip it in the bud. Maybe he should take some independent action. Maybe he could nip it, whatever it was, in the bud, before Mr. Bullard even heard about it.

Bullard had told him not to do anything unless Bullard said so. But he didn't get to be Kip

Carter by always doing what he was told, even by Mr. Bullard. He knew that Terry's gang of kids was down there. Most of them were girls or nerds. But Tank worried him a little. And Carly. He wanted some backup of his own. He made a couple of calls on his cell. Then he stepped out of the movie theater entry and walked down Main Street toward the café.

CHAPTER 41

Tank came into the café and said to Terry, "Kip Carter is outside with about four other guys. He wants to see you."

"No," Abby said.

Terry didn't say anything.

"We'll back you," Tank said. "Me and Carly, and I bet Steve would jump in."

"No," Abby said again.

Terry nodded slowly.

"Yes," he said.

"It's about me," Abby said. "Isn't it?"

"Yes," Terry said, "but it's about me too."

"I know who he has with him without looking," Abby said. "Tookie, Ray . . ."

"Yeah," Tank said.

"They are big mean guys, Terry," she said. "You don't need to do this. You don't need to defend my honor or whatever it is."

"It's my honor too," Terry said.

She felt desperate.

"Think, what would George say?"

"I think George would understand," Terry said.

He stood up. She stood with him. He patted her on the upper arm for a moment, then he turned and went out the front door of the café. Tank followed him. Abby stood frozen for a minute. Then she went after them, out the front door of the café, and, on the dead run, past them, and across Main Street toward the building where George had his gym.

Abby was right, Kip Carter's side was all football team. The kids had formed a big circle. Terry's side of the circle was more diversified. In the center of the circle was Kip Carter in a tank top and jeans. To Terry he looked like something out of *WWE SmackDown!* Terry walked into the middle of the circle and stood facing Kip Carter.

"I told you what would happen, you kept causing trouble," Kip Carter said.

Terry nodded.

"I want to know what you think you're doing bothering Mrs. Trent."

Terry shook his head.

"You better tell me now, Novak," Kip Carter said.

"Or what?" Terry said. "You try to beat up on Abby? Last fight you had with her, I heard she won."

Kip Carter seemed to freeze up for a moment. His face got red. He didn't speak.

He'll probably rush me, Terry thought. He could almost hear George's voice. *Keep him off with the jab. Cover up. Move.* Carter couldn't last long if he were swinging wild and off balance. *Nobody that strong,* George said. Even in boxing shape you can't be flailing with both hands and no feet under you and keep it up.

Out of the corner of his eye he saw George strolling across the street with Abby. George was talking, but Terry couldn't hear what he was saying. But George looked calm. It made Terry feel steadier.

"How's your lip," Terry said to Kip Carter.

And Carter rushed him. Terry went into his stance. Covered up. Crouched to make himself a smaller target. He moved right and stuck a jab out at Carter. Carter swarmed him, punching with both hands. Terry took most of them on his arms and moved back and jabbed again. He could hear George's voice. *Stick and move,* the voice was saying. *Stick and move.* He wondered if it was really George's voice. Kip Carter connected on a half-blocked roundhouse that staggered Terry. But Carter was off balance when he threw it, and all his weight wasn't in it. *Street fight, you don't want to break your hand on his head. Want to use the side of your fist if you can. Or your forearm. Elbow. Use your fists on his body.* Carter swung another big roundhouse left. Terry was able to lean back and check the punch past him with his right, block it hard with his left. He dropped a little lower and hit Carter hard with a right hook in his rib cage. He heard Carter grunt. He backpedaled and shuffled left while his head cleared. He could hear Carter's breath starting to rasp.

"Stand still and fight, you little freak," Carter gasped.

Terry kept circling left. His hands high, in a low crouch. It was odd how everything had come down to the fight. He didn't feel much. He didn't see much beyond Carter's movement before him. Carter was hitting him mostly on the arms and shoulders and he didn't really feel it. He was not aware of anyone around him. Of the kids standing in a circle. Of George standing with Abby. Of Paxton Bullard driving up behind the circle and easing himself out of his too-small car. All he saw was Carter, and only in a kind of faceless movement that he tracked and responded to without thought.

Carter tried to grab him with his right hand, but Terry stepped into him, which Carter didn't expect, and turned and blocked the right hand hard with both of his forearms. Then he drove his right elbow up and across, catching Carter on the cheekbone. Carter staggered. He followed with his left forearm, turning with the natural torque of the movements, and Carter staggered backward. His arms dropped and Terry, his feet still under him, holding his stance, hit him in the middle of the face with a straight right. And Carter went down. A kind of sigh went up softly from the circle of kids.

Carter stayed down for a moment, sitting on the ground. Then he struggled to his feet.

"I'll kill you," he gasped, and with his head down rushed at Terry.

Terry stepped aside. He heard George's voice through the murk of his intensity.

"Finish," George's voice said. "Finish it."

Carter came at him again, bull-rushing with his head down. Terry hit him with a left hook and then straightened him with the big uppercut George had taught him. It stopped Carter. He stood motionless for a moment, then slowly dropped to his hands and knees and stayed there, head hanging. There was no sound except for Carter's breath heaving painfully in and out.

Terry was still. As the fog of his intensity began to dissipate, he became aware that he was breathing hard. His hands would probably hurt in a while. He felt kind of bad for Kip Carter. He looked at Abby. He couldn't read her face. But there was no pleasure in it. He wasn't sure what it was. He looked at George. George nodded slightly. Terry understood that. He knew it was approval. George and Abby walked into the center of the circle. George squatted on his heels beside Kip Carter. He put a hand under Carter's chin and raised his head a little and looked at his eyes.

"How you feel?" George said.

Carter shook his head.

"Got a headache?" George asked.

Carter shook his head again.

"Follow my finger," George said, and moved his raised forefinger back and forth in front of Kip Carter's eyes.

"You dizzy?" George said.

"I . . . don't . . . think . . . so."

George nodded and stood up.

"He be all right," George said. "He more wore out than hurt."

Terry nodded slowly. Abby stood next to him without speaking.

"Lemme see your hands," George said.

Terry held them out.

"Nothing broken," George said.

Mr. Bullard pushed through the circle of kids. He stopped next to Carter and looked down at him, and shook his head slowly and made a sound as if he were spitting. Then he looked around the circle.

"Okay," he said. "What's going on here?"

"Come on to my place," George said to Terry. "We need to get some ice on your hands."

Terry nodded again and, with Abby, he followed George through the quiet circle of kids and across the street toward George's gym.

"Hey," Bullard shouted. "Don't you just walk away from me."

"Ice'll ease the swelling," George said. "Maybe won't hurt so much tomorrow."

They walked on. Bullard stared after them for a moment, then he turned toward the circle of kids, which had already started to thin.

"You all get out of here," he said. "Move!"

The remaining kids began to move. Kip Carter was on

one knee now, leaning on the other one. Bullard stood over him with his arms folded.

"Stand up," Bullard said scornfully, "and get in my car now."

Carter rose slowly and, still unsteady, moved carefully toward Bullard's car. Bullard stood for a moment staring after Terry, Abby, and George as they went into George's building. Then he turned on his heel and walked angrily toward his little car.

CHAPTER 42

Terry soaked his hands in ice water, taking them out periodically when the cold got too much. Abby watched him quietly.

"So," Terry said. "Whaddya think?"

"I didn't like it," Abby said.

George was stowing things: boxing gloves, trainer's tape, jump ropes.

"Would you have liked it better if Carter won?"

"No. I'd have hated it more," Abby said.

Terry was thrilled with his success, and the fact that Abby wasn't treating him like a hero was bothersome.

"He started it," Terry said.

"I know," Abby said.

"Well, you don't think he deserved it?" Terry said.

"I'm not thinking about Kip Carter," Abby said.

George picked up a couple of towels and tossed them in the hamper.

"I don't get it," Terry said. "I won the damn fight against the high school hero and you seem mad."

"I'm not mad," Abby said. "And I'm glad you won. I guess it just scared me a little."

"Hell," Terry said. "It scared me a little too. But it's over now. What's your problem?"

"If it had happened when he . . . bothered me in the woods," Abby said, "I would have been thrilled. I was so scared . . . and so mad . . . and you would have saved me from him."

"And this isn't saving you," Terry said.

"No," Abby said. "This is like revenge."

Terry stared at her.

"Well," George said. "Might be more than just revenge, might prevent him from bothering you again."

Abby nodded.

"I suppose," she said.

"Not a bad thing," George said.

"No."

"But that ain't what really bothering you, stuff about revenge."

"It's not?" Abby said.

George shook his head and grinned at her.

"You don't like the Terry Novak you saw in the fight. You never seen him before."

"He was so angry," she said. "He was, like, cruel."

"For god's sake," Terry said.

"Ain't gonna argue none about whether fighting's good or bad," George said. "My own guess is that it be good and bad, like most things. Hitting somebody is cruel, even if you have to do it. But say that you do have to do it, then being angry and cruel probably a good thing. Long as you control it."

"You think he had to fight?" Abby said.

"I think there are some things worth fighting 'bout," George said.

He grinned at her.

"I was Terry," George said. "You might be one."

Abby looked at Terry.

"But I don't know if I could spend my life with some-one cruel and angry like that," she said.

Terry felt the familiar electric thrill when she mentioned spending her life with him and the equally charged flicker of fear when she suggested there could be a reason not to.

George nodded.

"There it is," George said. "Isn't it?"

Terry and Abby both looked at him.

"You known him nearly your whole life," George said to Abby. "And you never seen him angry and cruel before."

"No."

"That the control thing," George said. "The good ones, like Terry . . ." *Wow!* Terry thought. "They can control it and use it only when they fight."

"And the bad ones?" Abby said.

"Kip Carter," George said.

"They don't control it," Abby said. "They let it out all the time."

George nodded.

"You think everybody has cruelty and anger in them?" Abby said.

"I hear you punched Kip Carter on the lip when he grabbed you in the woods," George said.

CHAPTER 43

In his office, in the now-empty school, Bullard loomed in front of Kip Carter.

"Nice going," Bullard said. "You've fixed it so now I'm going to have to do something about him. Her too, probably."

"I was trying to help," Kip Carter said.

"He beat you like a drum," Bullard said.

Kip Carter looked at the floor.

"A ninth grader . . ." Bullard said.

Kip Carter couldn't think of anything to say. He looked at the floor some more.

"You're yellow," Bullard said.

"Mr. Bullard," Kip said. "I'm not."

The veins in Bullard's neck were bulging. His face was red. His breathing was heavy and fast. His voice was hoarse.

"I told you not to touch him unless I said so," Bullard said. "Didn't I?"

Kip Carter nodded.

"But no, you jerk," Bullard said, "you had to be a hero. You thought you could beat him up easy, everybody thought you could beat him up easy. You even fooled me, but no more."

The color in Bullard's face deepened.

"You know why he beat you?" Bullard said. His voice was shaking.

"Because you quit," Bullard rasped. "Because he landed a couple of lucky punches and you folded like an accordion. I thought you were going to cry."

"I didn't quit, Mr. Bullard," Kip Carter said. "He beat me, but I didn't quit."

"You quit," Bullard said. "You think you can play in the Big Ten? You think a quitter like you can make the team? When I get through talking to the coaching staff out there, they won't give you a scholarship for cheerleading."

"My scholarship?"

"Forget about it. You go along with me, I go along with you. You only cross me once."

"I was trying to do the right thing for you, Mr. Bullard," Kip Carter said. "Novak was getting too close. I thought I could pound the fear of God into him."

"I don't care what you were trying to do," Bullard said. "You turned yourself into a joke. I got no use for a joke."

"And now you're going to ruin my scholarship."

"Absolutely."

"Mr. Bullard, I . . . You can't just throw me away . . . I know stuff."

"And you'll keep your mouth shut about anything you know," Bullard said. "Or you'll be swimming with the fishes like the other guy."

Despite the obvious rage he was in, Bullard's voice was suddenly quiet and hard as winter ice. Kip Carter realized he was seeing the Mr. Bullard that Jason must have seen, just before he died.

"Yes sir," Kip Carter said. "You can trust me, sir."

"And you can trust me," Bullard said. "You say one word and I'll bury you."

"Yes sir," Kip Carter said. "I won't say anything."

Bullard stared at him for a long time without speaking. Then he nodded slowly.

"No," Bullard said. "You won't."

Bullard jerked his head toward the door and Kip Carter turned and left. He appeared cowed and his head was down, but to himself he said, *The hell I won't.*

CHAPTER 44

Terry was through soaking his hands when Kip Carter walked into George's training room.

"Fight's over, son," George said to him.

"I don't want to fight," Kip Carter said.

Terry looked at him silently.

"So what do you want?" Abby said.

"I want to tell you about Mr. Bullard," he said.

Behind him the doorway was suddenly blocked by Bullard's huge frame.

"You three," he said. "Come with me."

"No," Terry said. "I want to hear what he has to say."

"He's got nothing to say and you three are coming with me."

Again Terry said, "No."

Bullard reached out and grabbed Terry by the front of his shirt and lifted him off the ground.

"No?" Bullard said. "No? You don't say no to me."

Abby made a little sound.

"Let go the boy, Mr..Bullard," George said.

Leaning against the wall with his arms folded, George was a sturdy middle-sized man, but he looked frail, Abby thought, compared to Mr. Bullard. Bullard let go of Terry and turned his head as if he had heard a fly buzz.

"What?" he said.

"Don't put your hands on the children," George said.

"Who the hell are you?" Bullard said.

"My name's George."

"Well, George." Bullard drew the name out so that it sounded mocking. "I am the principal of the high school, and these children are facing disciplinary action of a serious nature. If you stand there quietly and keep your mouth shut, you may not get into trouble."

"Talk to them right here," George said. "And don't touch them."

Bullard was trembling with partially contained rage. He looked volcanic.

"They're coming with me," Bullard said.

George shook his head.

"No? You're telling me no? You really think you can stop me?"

"Maybe so," George said.

Bullard spit on the floor in contempt.

"You three, now, come with me."

Terry, Abby, and Kip all said, "No," at the same time. Bullard's voice was thick, as if his throat was clogged.

"Then by God, I'll drag you out of here," Bullard said.

George stepped away from the wall and stood between the kids and Bullard. His arms were no longer folded. He held his hands relaxed in front of his chin, tapping his fingertips together lightly.

"Why don't you go someplace, Mr. Bullard," George said. "Have some tea. Take a shower. Calm down so's you won't do something crazy."

Bullard put his right hand out to shove George aside. George checked it aside with his own right and blocked it hard with his left.

"We don't really want to fight, do we, Mr. Bullard? Two grown men, in front of the kids?"

Bullard made a sound like a loud growl and lunged at George. George slid to his right and, as the lunge passed, knocked Bullard down with a right hook. Bullard sat down hard and looked startled for a moment. Then he growled again and struggled to his feet. Terry pushed Abby behind him to the wall and stayed in front of her. Kip Carter, too, got out of the way.

"Oh my god," Abby said.

Terry and Kip Carter said nothing.

George was in his boxer's stance now, hands protecting his head, arms and elbows protecting the body. His feet were in the right place.

"It's not too late, Mr. Bullard," he said. "We could stop here."

Bullard snarled and swung at George with a massive

fist. George blocked it and countered. George's hand movements were almost too fast to follow. Straight right, left to the body, right to the body, turning the hip, pushing off with his legs. Left hook to the head, right cross, left jab, and a brutal right uppercut that put Bullard down and kept him there. He wasn't exactly out, Terry thought. But he couldn't get his legs under him. It all took less than thirty seconds.

"I believe you saw this man assault me," George said.

They nodded.

"I think it's time to call the cops," George said.

Kip Carter went and stood over Bullard, looking down at him.

"He killed Jason Green," Kip said.

"Imagine the cops might be interested in that too," George said.

CHAPTER 45

They were in the Cabot police station with a Cabot police detective named Morris and a state police detective named Fogarty. Bullard was in another room with two other detectives. George was in the waiting room. Fogarty was doing the questioning.

"None of you is under arrest," Fogarty said. "You understand that? You are free to leave if you wish."

The three kids said they understood.

"You two are minors," he said to Terry and Abby, "so we'd rather not question you without your parents here. But I'd like to have you hear Carter's story, so when you have the proper adult supervision, you can comment on it."

Terry nodded.

Abby said, "Yes sir."

"But you," Fogarty said to Kip, "are eighteen. We will be very happy to listen to what you got to say."

"Sure," Kip said.

Morris clicked on a tape recorder.

"I'm Detective William Morris of the Cabot Police Department. We are taking a statement, voluntarily given by Kippen L. Carter, age eighteen, of Cabot, Massachusetts, a student at William Dawes Regional High School. The interview is being conducted with me by State Police Detective Lieutenant Alan Fogarty at Cabot, Massachusetts, Police Headquarters."

He gave the date and looked at Kip.

"You ready?" he said.

"Yes sir."

"Tell us your story," Fogarty said.

"Mr. Bullard, was, ah, a big football freak, you know? He was a big star in college and coulda gone pro but hurt his knee."

"Where?" Fogarty said.

"Where?"

"Where'd he go to college?"

"Illinois."

"University of?"

"Yes. He got me a scholarship there."

Terry and Abby sat side by side in the interrogation room listening. Terry had his hands folded in his lap. Abby rested her hand on Terry's forearm.

"And you were grateful," Fogarty said.

"Yes sir," Kip said. "He used to give us, the guys on the football team, the ones that were good, he used to give us steroids."

"Can you name what he gave you?"

"Not really," Kip said.

"Hard to remember," Fogarty said. "We'll come back to that later."

"We won the state super bowl last fall," Kip said.

"I'll need the names of the other kids getting steroids from Bullard," Fogarty said.

"Do I have to?" Kip said.

"'Fraid so, son," Fogarty said. "It's all out of the bottle now. There's no stuffing it back in."

Kip took in a deep breath.

"I gotta get through this," he said. "Can I give you a list, after?"

"Sure," Fogarty said.

"So one day he . . ."

"Bullard," Fogarty said.

"Yeah, Mr. Bullard, he brings me in his office and he says to me, how he helped me out with the 'roids and how he got me the scholarship to Illinois. And I say yes, like, I'm very grateful. And he says that the school is building a house, you know, the technical arts guys, and he says they need a little supervision, and would I be his man on the project? And I say sure, what am I supposed to do, and he says it's an experimental project and he doesn't want it talked about yet, and I'm to make sure none of the kids working on the project asks a bunch of questions or talks about it to other people, you know?"

"And you agreed," Fogarty said.

"Sure. It was easy, they were all scared of me . . ." Kip paused and looked at Terry. "Except him, I guess."

"What was the experiment?" Fogarty said.

"I don't think there was one. I think him and Mrs. Trent were building the houses and selling them and keeping the money."

"Mrs. Trent the current candidate for governor," Fogarty said.

"Yes."

"Why did you think it's a scam?" Fogarty said.

"Well, she was around a lot, and he was around a lot, and all the kids, me too, kept wondering what was going to happen to the house when it was done."

"Were there other houses?"

"I guess so. Some of the older kids say there were," Kip said.

"What happened to them?" Fogarty said.

"I don't know. I don't know even where they were built."

"Why do you think Mrs. Trent was involved?"

"She was there with him a lot. And sometimes they would, ah, sort of paw each other when they thought no one saw them."

"Who was the project supervisor?"

"Mr. Malcolm is head of the tech arts curriculum," Kip said. "I guess it was him. He wasn't around much. And the construction supervisor guys, they just knew about carpentry and wiring and stuff. Plus, you know, I was supposed to keep the kids from even asking."

Fogarty nodded slowly. He looked at Morris.

Then he said, "And what about Jason Green?"

There were two interrogation rooms in the Cabot police station. There was a one-way window in the wall between, and a speaker. The one-way window was adjustable in either direction. It was the first time since they had built the new station that there'd been occasion to use it. In the second room, where he could see through the window and listen on the speaker as Kip Carter told his story, sat Paxton Bullard. With him was a Cabot uniformed officer named Clarkson and a state detective named St. Germaine. Bullard's right eye was almost closed and his upper lip was swollen. He was slumped in his chair staring at the one-way window as if it were a television screen. He looked limp and smaller, as if he had been wrung out. He showed no response to Kip Carter's story.

"He called me on my cell," Kip Carter was saying. "Told me something had happened, and he needed my help, and to get my ass down to the beach."

"What time was this?" Fogarty said.

"'Bout 8:30?"

"And you went?"

"Oh yeah, I mean you didn't say no to Mr. Bullard . . ." Kip paused.

"And what?" Fogarty said.

"And . . . I guess I was kinda, um, flattered he asked me."

Fogarty nodded.

"Sure," he said. "Then what happened?"

"I went to the beach, and he said Jason had an accident and we had to get rid of the body.

"And I said, 'Why? Why don't we just call the cops?' And Mr. Bullard said people could see it as his fault. And I say I don't want no part of it. And he says, 'You know what's good for you, you'll do what I say.' And he gives me a look, *like . . . he was crazy. I was afraid not to do what he said."*

"So what did you do?" Fogarty said.

"Jason was lying with his face in the water. When we pulled him out, there was a big bruise on his face. I didn't like looking at him. I thought I was going to puke. I mean he was dead."

"Hard," Fogarty said. "Then what?"

"We put him in Mr. Bullard's trunk, and we took him to the Farragut Bridge, and we dumped him in. Mr. Bullard said by the time he washed up someplace, they couldn't tell how he died. And I said they could tell if he drowned or not. And Mr. Bullard said, he did drown."

St. Germaine got up and turned off the speaker. Bullard could still see Kip Carter talking, but he could no longer hear.

"We haven't arrested you yet," St. Germaine said. "But it's getting close. We're going to bring Mrs. Trent down here and talk with her. My guess is she'll dump it all on you."

Bullard was looking at the floor. He nodded slightly.

"So before you get lawyered up," St. Germaine said, "you want to tell us anything, might help your cause?"

Bullard shook his head slowly, still looking at the ground.

"Okay," St. Germaine said, "you're under arrest. Clarky, you wanna read him his rights?"

Clarkson took a small plastic laminated card from the breast pocket of his uniform shirt and began to read from it.

"You have the right to remain silent . . ."

CHAPTER 46

Fogarty walked out of the interview room with Terry and Abby.

"You kids got nothing to worry about," Fogarty said. "We'll need you to testify, but you haven't done anything bad, and a lot of what you did was good."

"What's going to happen to Kip?" Abby said.

"His father's on the way. We'll hold him until then and release him to his father. There any money?"

"His father's a doctor," Abby said.

"Okay. He stays with his story, which I take to be the truth . . ." Fogarty said.

"We do too," Abby said.

Fogarty nodded.

"All he's really guilty of is disposing of a dead body," Fogarty said.

"And being a really big jerk," Terry said.

"Lot of that going around," Fogarty said. "It's not

criminal. . . . He helps us fry the two big fish and hires a good lawyer, which is why I asked about the money, I suspect they'll work something out with the prosecutor and he won't have to do any time."

"Will you speak to somebody about him?" Abby said.

"If he stays on board with us," Fogarty said. "Yeah. I'll talk to the ADA on the case."

"What about Mr. Bullard and Mrs. Trent?" Terry asked.

"We'll arrest them both. If it goes the way these things often do," Fogarty said, "my guess is that it'll be a footrace to see which one can blame it all on the other one, and they'll implicate each other."

"I hope so," Abby said.

As they came into the waiting room, George stood.

"Waiting for these kids?" Fogarty said.

"I am," George said.

"You the guy gave Bullard the shiner?"

"I am," George said.

"I used to box a little," Fogarty said.

"I used to box a lot," George said.

Fogarty smiled and made a good-point gesture with his forefinger.

"On the other hand," Fogarty said, "I got a gun."

George smiled and made the same good-point gesture at Fogarty.

There was something going on between George and the big state cop. Something Terry didn't quite get. They were friendly, but they were circling each other a little, like two male dogs. Maybe the way tough guys were. He filed it.

"You teach this kid to box?" Fogarty said.

"Yes."

"Did a good job," Fogarty said. "Far as I can tell."

"I did," George said.

Wow!

Terry looked at Abby. She smiled at him.

"You got a gym in town?" Fogarty said.

"Yep."

"Maybe I'll come down and spar with you sometime."

George smiled.

"No guns," he said.

Fogarty smiled back.

"None," he said.

He looked at Terry and Abby.

"We'll be in touch," Fogarty said.

"Yes sir," Terry said.

Fogarty turned to George.

"These kids don't belong here," he said.

"That's correct," George said.

Fogarty shook hands with each of them.

Then he said to George, "So, get them out of here."

George nodded at Terry and Abby and the three of them left.

CHAPTER 47

They sat where they liked to sit, on the rocks, near the beach, where the sunlight was glistening on the water, which was a blue reflection of the cloudless sky, and the waves moved steady and restless, below them. There was a small breeze.

"I feel bad for Kip," Abby said.

"Kip?" Terry said.

"Yes."

"You never call him Kip," Terry said. "You always call him Kip Carter All-American. Like it was one big word."

"That was before I felt bad for him."

"Because he's in trouble?" Terry said.

"Yes, but not just that. Because he was like everybody else and he was trying so hard not to be."

"What's everybody else like?" Terry said.

There were some sailboats in the harbor, some tacking

back and forth, beating up into the wind, some with the sheet way out running straight before the wind.

"Kind of scared, not sure about what you should do, trying to fit in, hoping for a good future," Abby said. "You know."

"We're not like that," Terry said.

Abby didn't answer for a while. She watched the sailboats and felt the clean air from the ocean as she breathed.

Then she said, "No, we're not."

"So?" Terry said. "How come we're not like everybody else?"

Again Abby watched the ocean rolling out in front of her, out of the harbor, and across the Atlantic, and eventually lapping at the coast of Spain or someplace.

Finally she said, "We have each other."

Terry felt for a moment as if he were short of breath. *We have each other.* He breathed in the salt air until he felt calmer.

"We're fifteen," he said. "And we found each other already? Is that possible? Can you find somebody at fifteen?"

"Yes."

"And spend your life with them?" Terry said.

"Yes."

"And you know that, at fifteen?"

"Don't you?" Abby said.

"Yes," he said. "What about the boxing? You sounded like that was a problem."

"George made me understand," Abby said.

"By what he said about anger?"

"A little bit," Abby said. "But mostly by what he is."

"George boxed all his life," Terry said. "Did you see him take out Old Man Bullard?"

"And George is a good man," Abby said.

"Yes," Terry said.

"The best I ever met," Abby said.

"So if I grow up to be like George, we'll be fine?"

"Very fine," Abby said.

A herring gull swung down and landed near them on the rocks and looked for food. It found none. It looked at Terry and Abby. There was nothing there for it either. It turned and flew away.

"So," Terry said as they watched the bird fly off, "if we're going to be together, do you think you might get a butterfly tattoo on your butt?"

She smiled at him and put out her hand. He took it. They looked at each other.

Then Abby said, "How do you know I don't already?"

Turn the page for a preview of
Robert B. Parker's next book,

Chasing the Bear
A YOUNG SPENSER NOVEL

I was sitting with the girl of my dreams on a bench in the Boston Public Garden watching the swan boats circle the little lagoon. Tourists fed the ducks peanuts from the boats and the ducks followed them.

"It's a nice place," Susan said, "isn't it, to sit and do nothing."

"I'm not doing nothing," I said. "I'm being with you."

"Of course," she said.

The swan boats were propelled by young men and women who sat in the back of the boat and pedaled. The exact appeal of the swan boats had always escaped me, though I too felt it and had, upon occasion, gone for a ride with Susan.

We were quiet and I could feel her looking at me.

"What?" I said.

She smiled.

"I was just thinking how well I know you, and how close we are, and yet there are parts of you, parts of your life, that I know nothing about."

"Like?" I said.

"Like what you were like as a kid; it's hard to imagine you as a kid."

"Even though you have often suggested that I am still a kid, albeit overgrown?"

"That's different," Susan said.

"Oh?"

"I simply can't picture you growing up out there in East Flub-a-dub."

"Your geography has never been good," I said.

"Where was it?" Susan said.

"West Flub-a-dub," I said.

"I stand corrected," she said. "What was life like in *West* Flub-a-dub?"

"Where should I start, Doctor?"

"I know your mother died right before you were born by cesarean section. And I know you were raised by your father and your mother's two brothers."

"We had a dog too," I said.

"I think I knew that as well," Susan said. "Her name was Pearl, was it not, which is why we've named our dogs Pearl?"

"German shorthairs should be named Pearl," I said. "So what else would you like to know?"

"There must be more you can tell me than that," Susan said.

"You think?" I said.

"I think," Susan said. "Talk about yourself."

"My favorite topic," I said. "Anything special?"

"Tell me about what comes to your mind," she said. "That will sort of tell us what you think is important."

"Wow," I said. "Being in love with a shrink is not easy."

"But well worth the effort," Susan said.

"Well," I said.

Susan leaned back on the bench and waited.

My father and my uncles were carpenters and shared a house. They all dated a lot, but my father never remarried, and my uncles didn't get married until I left the house. So for me growing up it was an all-male household except for a female pointer named Pearl.

Parents' Day at school was a sight. They'd come, the three of them, all over six feet, all more than two hundred pounds, all of them hard as an axe handle. They never said a word. Just sat there in the back of the room, with their arms folded. But they always came. All three.

My father boxed and so did my uncles. They'd pick up extra money boxing at county fairs and smokers. They began to teach me as soon as I could walk. And until I could take care of myself, they took care of me . . . pretty good.

Once when I was ten, I went to the store for

milk and coming home, I passed a saloon named The Dry Gulch. Couple of drunks were drinking beer on the sidewalk. They said something, and I gave them a wise guy answer, so they took my milk away and emptied it out. One of them gave me a kick in the butt and told me to get on home.

When I got home, I told my uncle Cash, who was the only one there. One of them was always there. Cash asked me if I was all right. And I said I was. He asked me if I might have been a little mouthy. I said I might have been. Cash grinned.

"I'm amazed to hear that," Cash said.

"But I didn't say anything real bad."

"Course you didn't," Cash said.

"One of them kicked me," I said.

Cash nodded.

"I'll keep that in mind," he said. "And when Patrick and your father come home, we'll straighten things out."

When they got home, Cash and I told them about what happened. Patrick and my father and Cash all exchanged a look, and my father nodded.

Patrick said, "If you saw him again, could you point out the guy who kicked you?"

"Sure," I said.

"Let's go down and take a look," my father said.

So all of us, including the dog, went down to The Dry Gulch and walked in.

"Sorry, pal," the bartender said to my father. "Can't bring that dog in here."

My father said to me, "See any of the people that gave you trouble?"

I nodded.

"Which ones?" my father said.

"You hear me?" the bartender said. "No dogs."

There were six guys drinking beer together at a big round table. I pointed out two of them. My father nodded and picked me up and sat me on the bar.

"Which one kicked you?" he said.

"The one in the red plaid shirt," I said.

My father looked at Patrick.

"You want him?" my father said.

"I do," Patrick said.

"Yours," my father said.

"Mister," the bartender said. "Maybe you don't hear me. Get that dog out of here . . . and get the damn kid off the bar."

Without even looking at him, my father said, "Shut up."

Pearl sat down in front of the bar near my feet. All the men at the round table were staring at us. My two uncles walked over and leaned against the wall, near the round table. Patrick was looking at the man in the red plaid shirt.

My father walked over to the round table.

"You," he said to one of the men. "Step out here."

"What's your problem?" the man said.

"I don't have a problem," my father said, "you do, and it's me."

"That kid been crybabying about me?" the man said.

"That kid is my son," my father said. "The gentlemen leaning on the wall are his uncles. We're here to kick your ass."

The man looked at his five friends and stood up.

"Yeah?" he said.

They all stood up. My father hit the man and the fight started. Pearl and I stayed quiet, watching. Behind me, I heard the bartender calling the police.

By the time the cops arrived, both the men who had teased me were out cold on the floor. The man in the red plaid shirt was lying outside on the sidewalk. I don't quite know how that happened, except that my uncle Patrick had something to do with it. The other three guys were sitting on the floor looking woozy.

The cop in charge, a sergeant named Travers, knew my father.

"Sam," he said. "You mind telling me what you boys're doing?"

"They harassed my kid on the street, Cecil," my father said. "Stole his milk."

Travers nodded and looked at the bartender.

"I believe I been telling you, Tate," he said, "to keep the drunks inside the saloon."

"They got no call to come in here and beat up my customers," the bartender said.

"Well," Travers said. "They got *some* call. Your kid gets bothered by a couple drunks, you got some call."

He looked around the room and then at my father.

"Maybe not this much call," he said. "Probably gonna get fined, Sam."

"Worth the money," my father said.

Travers smiled.

"Known it was you three," he said, "I'd have brought more backup."

"Ain't supposed to bring no dog in here either," the bartender said. "Board of Health rule."

"We'll go hard on them 'bout that," Travers said.

My father came over and took me off the bar.

"Probably have to appear in court to pay the fine," Travers said.

"Lemme know," my father said.

He walked toward the door. Pearl and I followed him. My uncles closed in behind us.

And we left.

Chapter 4

"How come he didn't arrest you?" I said to my father when we got home.

"Known Cecil most of my life," my father said.

"But wasn't it against the law?" I said. "What you did?"

"There's legal," my father said, "and there's right. Cecil knows the difference."

"And what you did was right," I said.

"Yep. Cecil would have done it too."

"How you supposed to know that what you're doing is right?" I said.

"Ain't all that hard," my uncle Patrick said. "Most people know what's right. Sometimes they can't do it."

"Or don't want to," Cash said.

"But how do you know?" I said.

My father sat back and thought a minute.

"You can't know," he said. "But you think about it before you do it, if you got time, and then you trust yourself."

"How 'bout if you don't have time to think and you done it and it was wrong?" I said.

"Did it," my father corrected me.

He was a bear for me saying things right. Even when he didn't always say it right himself. When he wasn't around, I talked like all the other kids talked, and I think my father knew that. As long as I knew how to talk right, then I could choose.

"Sometimes you make a mistake," he said. "Everybody does."

"It sounds too hard," I said. "How do I know I can trust myself?"

"It'll be pretty much instinct," my father said. "If you been raised right."

"How do I know I'm being raised right?" I said.

My father looked at my uncles. All three of them smiled.

"None of us knows that," my father said.

I nodded. It was a lot to think about.

"How 'bout, what's right is what feels good

afterwards," my father said. "It's in a book, by a famous writer."

My father wasn't educated. Neither were my uncles. And they didn't know what they were supposed to read. So they read everything. Not long after I was born, my father bought a secondhand set of great books, bound in red leather, and he and Patrick and Cash used to take turns reading to me every night before bed. None of them had any idea what was considered appropriate for a little kid. They just took turns plowing on through the classics of Western literature in half-hour chunks every night. I didn't understand most of it, and I was bored with a lot of it. But I loved my father and my uncles, and I liked getting their full attention.